Natasha IllumBerg was born in Sweden and grew up there and in Denmark and now lives in Tanzania. She is the only female licensed hunter in East Africa and specializes in buffalo safaris. Her previous book, *Rivers of Red Earth*, tells the story of her journey to becoming a professional hunter. She is presently at work on her next book, a novel, which will be published in England in 2006.

For automatic updates on Natasha IllumBerg visit harperperennial.co.uk and register for AuthorTracker.

Praise for *Tea on the Blue Sofa*:

'This slender yet unsentimental tribute to friendship and the devastation of loss before love has scarcely got into its stride could become an African classic. Natasha IllumBerg captures the essence of who Tonio was, without imprisoning him on a page. The dedication of *Tea on the Blue Sofa* speaks volumes to me, his mother'   ERROL TRZEBINSKI

'The bravest of the brave, the most generous of the generous. It takes real courage both to love as deeply and to write as well as Natasha IllumBerg. Her memoir of a love that died before it could be born already deserves to be called a classic'
                                    FIAMMETTA ROCCO, *Economist*

'Well written . . . Painstakingly honest'   *Daily Telegraph*

NATASHA ILLUMBERG

Tea on the Blue Sofa

*Whispers of love and longing
from Africa*

HARPER PERENNIAL
London, New York, Toronto and Sydney

Harper Perennial
An imprint of HarperCollins*Publishers*
77–85 Fulham Palace Road
Hammersmith
London W6 8JB

www.harperperennial.co.uk

This edition published by Harper Perennial 2005

First published in Great Britain by Fourth Estate 2004

Copyright © Natasha IllumBerg 2004
PS section copyright © Louise Tucker 2005, except
'That Fickle Chum Time'
by Natasha IllumBerg © Natasha IllumBerg 2005

PS™ is a trademark of HarperCollins*Publishers* Ltd

Natasha IllumBerg asserts the moral right to
be identified as the author of this work

A catalogue record for this book
is available from the British Library

ISBN 978-0-00-717870-4

Typeset in Linotype Giovanni Book
by Palimpsest Book Production Limited, Polmont, Stirlingshire

For you. As promised.

TEA ON
THE BLUE SOFA

Such grown-up tears roll down relentlessly, when *moley*, milky eyes still only know how to turn up, hoping for the blurry light of a mother's face.

Such fine nails on a new foot. Each of the five, already with its own half-moon, rising out of toes that cannot even support the weight of a person yet.

How soon would the nails bend over those toes, if not cut? And dig in to the ground, like crows' claws, clasping the soil already from the first steps.

Such beautiful hair on the head of that child, so quickly it grows long. Falling fair strands. Seems it grows faster down, than the child up.

The earth is sucking hard from underneath.

Waiting, sucking.

1

1

My mother once met a dead tiger. In Margali, India. Four years before I was born. She walked up to its still-warm body with timid steps, wary of cutting its camouflaging protection from the shades and shadows – seeing the whole clearly the first time. Aware that only its death will let you cut a tiger out of the jungle. She was overcome by sadness. In an attempt to find a way to carry with her some of the strength lost in the death of a tiger, she and my father cut out the heart and ate it. Bearing in mind the stories my grandfather told about his times in India, my father knew that they were not the first to do such a thing. If there is strength in anything, it must be in a tiger's heart.

*   *   *

'I have two mindsets, that can be exchanged like keyboards, with letters of different languages. The mind of a writer, and the mind of a hunter. But you bring me straight back to the hunter's mind,' I had written to you, as we became losers to the shade-clad eyes of the world for falling in love. 'Eyes, ears, taste. Legs aching to walk, or to stop, or not knowing which, but aching. Salt at the corners of my mouth. The hope of an opportunity for a shot at the top of the heart. Pursuit, following tracks with expectation, alertness and a bit of fear.'

'The shot at the top of the heart,' you answered, 'has already happened. My heart has been severed from all reason. You can do with it what you want. You see the flower has been pollinated. This process cannot be reversed, and that is that. Nobody will ever have the power to remove these feelings, not even you.'

You left this world, on your way to my embrace.

In waiting for my eyes to get used to the dark, morning broke and daylight let me down.

Dawn entered as well-meaning and out of place as a mime for children and I never liked them much. In their lack of sound they throw unwanted desperation into communication.

I went out on the gravel road, where your beautiful body had fallen, brutally murdered by a single shot to the heart. The cruelty of that. The heart. The head would have been a different story, but the heart, my love. The heart that appeared on everything.

I lay down in the road next to the last part of you I would ever see, and hated myself for understanding that it had run out of your heart. A hunter knows at a glance.

A few drops of your heart's blood, I put on my lips.

I was never allowed to see you again, or to go to your funeral, but a bit of your strength, a few drops of the heart that was on everything, I will carry with me to death, a lifetime later, not now.

And the thick window that is between myself and my bitter-cold grief, between my life and your death, opened a little.

2

The first letter was sent from me to you. It was a Tuesday. You took it as a confirmation, you told me later. A confirmation that I was the person who you had hoped I might be, ever since we met several years ago.

I still had a base in Kenya then. We had had Tanzanian tea on my blue sofa for the first time, the day before I sent the letter. It was a sofa larger than any sofa I had ever seen before, well, not longer, but deeper than any sofa, any of us, really, had ever seen before. It was a special kind of blue, three different-coloured threads especially chosen and woven together, to make the perfect blue. A child's blue pulled out again after years in the attic, a child's forgotten blue with a thread of time's dust woven into it.

I wrote to you that I had found a seed pushed in between the cushions of the sofa after you had left. That it must had dropped out of your trouser pocket at some stage, when we were talking and drinking tea. I told you I had planted it and could not wait to see what would become of it.

The answer you sent back was as if you had finally discovered me, caught me in the act of being somebody you had already made a space for in your heart. You shouted, 'I knew it!'

But as far as airborne words are concerned, you had already started using them years ago. Back then, you had seen me sitting by the fireplace at a friend's house, seated in my usual position of people-watching. Watching people was what I would spend most of my evening doing, at any kind of social gathering. Watching intensely and stubbornly, slightly embarrassed that I had still not understood the rules of this game I had so often witnessed. Confused at my own inability to comprehend the point of the sport I was obviously (at least in body) part of, somehow.

You came over and crouched down, knees and bent toes resting on the floor, beside my armchair. 'You look like a bird of prey,' was the first thing you said to me that day. 'I don't know which kind, but it is a raptor.'

I didn't find those words interesting in any way, I didn't. I didn't trust them. I told you to tell me a story, instead of trying to flatter me. I was a bit tired of the enormously long and invisible suffixes written in lemon juice, that so often appear later when strangers' sentences are held up to the sunlight.

I didn't see you for quite a while after that. Well, I met you on occasions, but didn't talk to you and didn't see you more than I see anything big so close without taking a step away from it first.

Children have understood so clearly, that we cease to exist when we close our eyes. As grown-ups we only understand when we see in the rear-view mirror.

I was born without eyelids so sooner or later I had to let you in. I couldn't keep on turning my face away. But you had known that we existed, before I had seen. Thank God for that. There would not have been any time at all for us otherwise.

Of course I don't accept time like most people any more. I can't. To live in some kind of social society we have to accept the clock, ageing, the rising and setting of the sun and the changing seasons, but we don't have to accept the value of time on the scale of a clock. I don't. I never have. Thank God for that too, my love. Clocks spat on us.

Then I met you at a party again, at the same house. At the house of the same beautiful woman, a friend who lives in a labyrinth. Honouring the masquerade theme, you looked like a Cossack – in a huge white sheepskin hat. Perhaps bought on the road to Naivasha. And you had in turn honoured the Cossacks with your vodka consumption. Red-label Smirnoff, certainly not blue.

I spent most of my time leaning against a Masai spear, with a drink in my other hand, enjoying the evening as it floated past my friends and me. I caught a glimpse of you out of the corner of my eye, hovering closer as the night went by, until you caught me standing on my own.

You said, 'You are always there somewhere at the back of my mind. I met you the first time many years ago. I remember what you wore. Then we met several times again, but we never had the chance to talk properly. Still you are there, in my mind.'

'Yeah, yeah,' I said, laughingly putting one hand on your shoulder. A cloud of a sulkiness passed over your face. 'Why don't you come and tell me if we chance to meet in the dukas[1] on a Monday morning?'

You sat down, trying to look more sober and we talked of books and paintings, the sea and the bush.

And silken lines were drawn between words and paint, the hunting of buffaloes and the catching of waves.

Monday morning you arrived at my gates, gardenia intact in your inner pocket.

Now I must learn to suppress the overwhelming hunger or even greed for a future that will not be.

To ignore that greed death offers.

There was such a relief in us both when we had finally understood what was the only way in life: to not be too greedy for each other – to not own too much too quickly. To let taste buds be just that, instead of letting greed open demanding mouths wide in hungry expectation. To keep from letting taste buds open helplessly, with only withering in sight shortly. You more than I had tried that so many times before. But I knew the feeling too. Looking over your shoulder in fear of the other person's sticky eyes and their purple-faced fright of losing something they never owned in the first place.

'To cut the ropes of two boats,' you called it 'and find the absolute happiness in discovering that they end up on the same shore by pure force of nature, not force of guilt, fear or confusion.'

Finally there.

Finally there.

No doubts.

'No gaps' was your way of saying it.

Boiled is what I hate, boiled, boiled, boiled, rolled around with other bits and pieces inside people's worlds of numerous tasteless root vegetables and genuine chicken stock. Until one thing is no longer distinguishable from another.

There are so many now who think they know about us, so many who thought they knew everything about your heart, because of your past, but we both knew that and laughed. So many who think they know anything about my half-Danish half-Swedish heart because of the way I carry my feet forward.

Steamed. Our colours enhanced and bodies slightly softened, by heat travelling upward, individual shape intact, nothing important thrown out with the water. We were on our way, we had already started our journey, ropes *are* cut.

They were lies, the pictures I saw of you in the newspapers just the other day. In them your face was falling, like bitter almonds from a tree. But it was a lie; you didn't look like that any more. Your face had changed. I saw it happen.

The stories you told me about waking up full of deep fear and confusion next to a prostitute with black plastic hair in Mombasa, were obvious. (The same kind of plastic that is wrapped around most electric wires.) There had been so many lies.

Lost in black gaping holes.

You forgot if you were looking for a way in or out. I love you for telling me, but I would have guessed anyway. It was written all over your face when I met you.

You never entered my house without a gardenia. You pulled it out amazingly intact from an inner pocket, always stating it was the most beautiful gardenia you had ever seen. Much more beautiful than all the others you had given me before. They were your favourite flower. When you were born, the room you were in with your mother was filled with the scent of gardenias and you told me the story of your maternal grandmother's gardenia bush. A bush grown from a cutting, planted at the Kenyan coast. When she left Kenya, to go back to England, that particular bush was given to your family and planted in your garden at Shanzu. On the way to some white swings. By the thought of that now, I imagine them swinging, empty, not fast, not slow, but continuous. Swinging fruitlessly. When your grandmother died, you told me, her ashes were spread around it and from then on it would flower every year on her birthday without fail. The third of December. Then the bush was moved and never flowered again. Some things don't like to be moved, I know. But to you, it stopped flowering because the ashes of your grandmother were not there to remind it any more.

You mostly arrived on a motorbike.

I could hear your smile from behind the helmet.

Eyes wide open, two steps up until inside my house. Expectation, the sound of the zip on your jacket. And then tea, on the blue sofa. First the kitchen, to wait for the water to boil as we moved around the table in the middle, in a gravitationless space of drying bread and ripening mulberries, just picked from the tree outside. Polite conversation initially, with me glancing at your hands. How I loved your hands. They were the most

13

beautiful I ever saw. One crossed over the other, or one holding the wrist of the other, resting in front. Or a hand before your mouth as you laughed. There was nothing pure about your hands at all, just real.

And then tea on the blue sofa. You sitting back, me putting my feet up on the sofa. The preparation of it all. You told me later that you knew for sure, when you saw me undo my shoes, before I folded my legs that first time. I never quite understood that.

Now imagine an egg. Perfectly sealed and slightly pointed. A white egg balancing on a steel-clean surface. It is there simply because of the wonder of nature. So strong it is in its rightness, so clearly outlined against the air around it. If I lay it in my hand, across my life-line and close my first around it, I won't be able to crush it. I simply can't, it is the wonder of physics. But I don't touch this egg, I leave it there and marvel.

Just slightly above this still life, a giant pendulum swings back and forth. Comparative to the egg, it is the size and material of a tank. *THE INFINITE NO* is the name of the pendulum, and it swings with such uncontrolled power, such limitlessness. There is the *INFINITE NO* travelling back and forth as if on patrol to crush, or cut time in bite-size pieces, just at fingernail-distance above the perfect egg on a spotless surface.

In that centimetre of air between the egg and the pendulum, is all hope, are endless possibilities – the reality of that hope, however, is a matter of millimetres, one way or the other.

3

Do you remember the bees? The strange swarms of bees that kept coming. Thousands of them. I opened the windows in my bedroom and they flew in. The first time they found their way into my bedroom on their own, the next time I had to invite them by opening all four windows. They were so calm and friendly and landed in clusters – one hanging from the opening in the mosquito-net around my bed and another in one of the window frames. I couldn't close my window for days. At night a few stayed inside my closed net, I knew they meant no harm. These bees were acting strangely; they weren't so alive that they were busy stinging them-selves to death. I liked having a house that big swarms of bees would circumnavigate and enter through cracks and openings. The fact that they all got weaker and eventually fell down dead on the floor one by one, was the part I chose to not take seriously.

It happened three times in a week Margaret, my giant soft-spoken Kamba[2] maid, kept sweeping them out, without any sign of surprise or inquisitiveness about the one room in the house that kept filling up with bees. Her serious sweeping made me laugh and I used it as a picture later, in one of my letters to you.

As you remember I started off saying, 'Maybe we will be together one day,' and then it became, 'maybe we will be together in twenty-five years'. You used to get so cross when I said that, you hated it and refused to express any kind of amusement at the thought. You were not the kind of person who would let a piece of chocolate melt in your hand. Or a piece of ice – strange, all those newspapers would call me that later. You see our love was all a bit frightening at first. For several reasons. I was with another man who had since long chosen to become my best friend as opposed to a lover, but I still thought I would hurt him frightfully by being the first to let go. I was wrong. After we parted he turned to another woman without the slightest pause. He only ever once met me after that. He made the meeting as brief as possible and then, very strangely, handed me a bunch of cigars on his way out from the room I had taken in a hotel for squirmishly chirpy Kilimanjaro climbers. For months I kept coming across the silver holsters of Romeo y Julieta amongst my shoes and clothes.

There is nothing I could have done or wanted to do to stop you from becoming my life's love. The heart is the heart, but it mattered to try to square things with a man I had spent so many years with. I needed to look him in the eyes and tell him that I had moved on as soon as he came back, I didn't want to do it over the telephone. It looks so childish now that I have lost my love and my best friend forever. Disaster, pain and death swallowed us all up anyway.

I had tried; I tried to push you away, until both of us settle our affairs. I even tried convincing myself that it was just lust at first. Of course you wouldn't stay away and the emotions I tried to calm with fragments of self-deceit in the form of simple indulgences were getting totally out of control.

With fear I watched myself search for solutions far more likely than true love. Love would always deprive me of my freedom. That was before we laughingly understood that it was a fear we had always both had. The fear of not being close enough when close, and not far enough apart when apart, yet always together.

I lay on my bed one afternoon whispering to the bees, who by then knew most of my thoughts, as they flew in and out of my bedroom,

'Ja visst gör det ont när knoppar brister. Varför skulle annars våren tveka? Varför skulle all vår heta längtan

19

bindas I det frusna bitterbleka? Höljet var ju knoppen hela vintern . . .'[3]

With a teacup in your right hand and one in my left, searchingly as if I didn't know whether I was to find gold or a land-mine, I probed my way forward one Thursday until I found myself completely lost in love. I wanted to say, but I couldn't, not yet.

The cracking of denial makes a hell of a noise to one's own ears from inside the space woven to protect soft-skinned change from prying eyes.

A cat was let out of a bag. Out it jumped, wild-eyed, disoriented, pupils gone mad with darkness. A simple, wild cat really. But smart, oh very smart. Quickly it assesses the situation. Fortunately it has a sense of humour, it can see the tragic, the painful, but also the funny in being a cat let out of a bag. Now let's watch it. Let's watch it compose itself, lick its ruffled fur into place. As any cat would, as any cat should really. It is OK that it will eventually utterly compose itself. Soon it is a cat of the world, like it used to be, before this wretched sack business. It might even get a walking-stick.

Eventually the event will be forgotten. Forgotten is the look of fright and panic on its face, forgotten is how terribly savage it looked. A cat of utter elegance with only one subtle fear that nobody knows about any more.

I thought I had everything under control.

*   *   *

20

A week later, when I went to let you out of my house, I could not look into your eyes. You asked if I was angry with you about something. I answered the next day. I told you that it had been something far worse I had tried to keep concealed that midday. Much worse, in its most ironic sense. Not kept hidden like a present, which only at first is charmingly hidden in a box. A present promises revelation, and the biggest feeling of all; expectation! To be followed no doubt by the clapping of excited hands and a moment or many moments of unfearful gratitude and balance.

I tried merely in the most practical sense to protect what was so naked, pigment-free. An albino emotion, with a desperate need to set out in search for the lightest spot possible.

'I don't know what we will let life bring us,' I said, 'but until we do I will just clutch this feeling to my chest. Crossed arms, holding it close, keeping it from burning. Telling it to half-close its red tearful eyes. For no other reasons than I selfishly adore it.'

So finally, I let go and told you that I had found Margaret sweeping out the years one morning. That I had woken up that day to wide-open doors and clouds of years being swept out into the morning breeze before I could stop her. I told you to blame it all on my giant maid. You told me you didn't dare to, so we better just accept it. 'Until the moment we can be together,' I wrote, 'I shall just try to breathe in, breathe out. All in a steady rhythm. I shall imagine my chest as a balloon being blown up by a purple-faced child who doesn't have the capacity to ever get past that hard point. So it tries again and again and again. Breathe in, breathe out.'

But that all happened much later.

When I was already yours.

I have always been slightly shocked by the dishonest way English people sign off their letters. 'Yours' they will write to a person they hardly know. The English have such a rich language yet they sign off letters like this to more or less any kind of person with no meaning to their life. Perhaps they have too many words to appreciate them.

But to me words have a literal meaning. I often signed off my letters to you 'Yours'. Of course you understood immediately.

'Don't you love the expression "to watch one's words"?' I wrote to you. 'I know I have to do that. I line them up with great difficulty. But then if I turn my back for ever so slight a moment (and how can I avoid that?), it all goes horribly wrong. They start running in all directions. I try to catch them but they slip so easily from my grip. "Curiosity" runs in one direction. "Desire" in the other. Damn! There goes beautiful "elbow" as quick and heading in the same direction as "thirst", already halfway over the hill. They have done it again! All gone, with an exception of some miserable word like "moist". (Standing big-eyed in front of me pleading to be used.) Of course I am not surprised about their behaviour, they are my words after all. But I have to try to watch them better!'

Then you would ring me to ask for words for your paintings and I would ring you and ask for pictures for my words. 'Turn on a penny, staccato on short legs,' were my words for a buffalo painting. And the pictures you gave my words came wrapped in things like an ever-flowering gardenia, giant palm leaves shimmering on one side, like mother-of-pearl and other images I had never seen before. Like 'the configuration', as you very seriously called the large cluster of freckles I have on the back of my right leg. I was born with this mark, yet you were the first person ever to find it. When I was a shorts-clad child, in pale Swedish summer nights, grown-ups would occasionally catch me as I ran by, to brush off what they thought was dirt from the lawn or from a tree. As a hunter in shorts, in Tanzania, my friends in the bush always seem to think I have walked into a cloud of giant pepper-ticks. To everyone it always looked like something that should be brushed off or pulled off with tweezers. Yet you, you as the first and only person, were seriously surprised that I had lived with this for thirty years without realizing the obvious truth about the skin on the back of my right leg. The 'right-in-your-face, can't-miss-it-obvious' truth. To you, this thing that all my life I had so ignorantly disregarded simply as an odd and rather ugly birthmark, was a drawing. Very clearly a drawing of a lion, a bicycle, and a nondescript character riding the lion. I had to lie on my stomach on the blue sofa one afternoon, as you sat on the floor with a torn-off piece of newspaper, a black pen and your nose about one centimetre above the mark, trying to keep me from twisting and turning too much, in laughter or curiosity to see.

The relief, to finally have found the person who thought the same things important and worth attention. For the first time we were sharing the world of unimportant things that the uninterested call 'details', and arrogantly discarding things that we had both been told were important but had never felt were so.

You never told me I split hairs. You understood I didn't. I just needed to tell the stories exactly, exactly as I felt them. Or understand the story exactly as somebody else felt it. What is the point of words if we don't try to use them carefully, precisely? How are we to say that we understand each other then? There aren't enough words as it is.

You have to try to get to the core, to the marrow in communication and in life. Blood buzzing in the fingertips is the whole point.

It wasn't that I had never loved before. I had. We both had. Past love wasn't a lie, not at all, I just had never expected to find you, my love. I thought people weren't meant ever to feel so fulfilled by one person.

24

When I was a child I had accepted that nobody would ever be able to understand me fully and that I would perhaps never understand them fully either. Always slightly on the edge of any social group, my closest friends were my dog and a particular tree. To them I would talk to for hours. I was never sad or angry about being slightly outside, I accepted it as my fate and made it into my strength. But now that you are gone, my love, I feel loneliness spreading through my body, I watch it stretching out its little crooked arms inside me. Like the globule of ink on my desk that was contained in its own perfect voluptuous circle until just a moment ago, when a drop from under my teacup fell right on top of it and made it run in all directions.

I wake up at night with nowhere to go, no promises to keep and no whispers any more.

4

The first time I heard the whisper was when I was about six years old. I remember it very clearly.

My parents had gone away. I would guess they had driven from our home in Blekinge in Sweden, to Sealand, Denmark. Perhaps to visit one of my grandmothers or perhaps they had been invited to a dinner or a shoot somewhere. I love to imagine my mother wearing her red silk dress with white squares on it as she jumped into the Range Rover just before leaving. My mother's hair at its bounciest, my father's at its flattest. Scent and kisses.

I was to stay with the gamekeeper, Mr Persson, and his not-quite-wife Mrs Svensson, who helped my mother in our home. This wasn't the first time I had stayed and

I would have waved my parents goodbye thinking, that I might, if I was lucky, already this afternoon start indulging in the culinary advantages there were for a six-year-old staying with Mr Persson and Mrs Svensson. White bread baked with syrup, Bob's divine apricot jam in a jar big enough to lose your knife in. And hopefully, very hopefully if I was lucky we might get crispy pieces of fried ham with apple sauce for supper, things I would never get at home. The mere luxury of eating pork as opposed to some kind of deer meat from the estate was something I only experienced very occasionally; at school, at my grandmother's house and at the gamekeeper's. 'Fläsk', as it is called in Swedish, in little square pieces, fried hard and golden-brown.

There are some particular moments that I carry with me from my visits to their little red house that smelt of frying pans and geraniums.

I remember being told that Mrs Svensson's eldest son P had once fallen into the nettles outside their house and had been stung all over his back. I considered him a hero because of that.

Summer afternoons in their garden. Sneaking a spoof lump of sugar into Mrs Svensson's coffee. We were seated on the lawn just in front of all her nettles, and I told her to watch the surface of her coffee (a moment later a tiny plastic figure of a naked person would float to the surface and I would laugh hysterically).

Then there were the dirty magazines in their loo.

With wooden shoes, and a sponge of a mind, I would sit quietly and rather longer than expected on their loo and discover the secrets of the adult female body as it, literally, unfolded in front of me.

But one of the things I remember most clearly was the 'whisper'.

Mrs Svensson had put me to bed in one of their two bedrooms. The room that used to belong to P and T – her sons. They had both left home by now and I could pick either bed in which to sleep. I chose the one next to the window. It was only glass, wall and a few steps away from the owls my father had put in a huge aviary behind Mr Persson's house. In the evening I was put to bed, and eventually Mrs S and Mr P switched off all lights and went to bed upstairs.

I had been fast asleep hours later, when suddenly I woke up.

I felt a hand caressing my cheek ever so gently. It was obvious to me that nobody was in the pitch-black room, but I wasn't afraid. It was natural and very loving. Then a whisper in that particular tone and voice. 'Anoushka . . .' said in an urgent way, as if to say, 'Look here, here I am.'

That was the first time I heard it. From then on I would wake up about three times every year to that urgent whisper. Never the touch again, but the word and the whisper that followed me until I was about thirty and a half.

The last time I heard the whisper, it came from your lips. I had never told you about it. I don't think I had ever told anybody about it. It was just one of those things that was in my picture of reality, because I had heard it the first time at a stage of my life when the world to me was so full of incomprehensible things anyway and I had been taught by grown-ups to believe them whether I understood them or not. It had followed me since I was six years old, I didn't think about it. Not until I picked up the phone a few days before you died and heard you say it. The same particular way of saying it, the same whisper. Now it is about six months since you left and I haven't heard the whisper again.

I wake up at night with nowhere to go, no promises to keep and no whispers any more. The night has gone solid and when I stretch in the mornings it is to push the walls away.

Clip, clap, clippedy-clap, I miss my wooden shoes.

I had hardly had time to fall in love with you before you had swallowed my soul. My reaction time was longer than yours – I was always catching up – so seeds we planted in me keep growing now, and there is nothing I can do to stop them. The weather is gone but my season cannot be halted. Leaves keep unfolding for us, all in vain, like fair hair that keeps growing on an ever-stilled head.

I had tried to resist our love at first, tried to push it

away, it was so much larger than me, so out of my control, I did all I could to make myself stop it all, but I knew.

I knew when I woke up with you sitting on the floor next to my bed. You had brought sushi to my house that evening. Flying-fish eggs like pieces of sand inflated far beyond solidity, millions of tiny 'pops' waiting to happen. We drank sake and discussed your ideas behind the paintings you were going to start making. Your photographs of Kenyan butcher-shops lay spread all over my buffalo table. I drank far too much sake, we both did, but I wasn't as accustomed to it as you were, and a few hours later I ended up almost falling asleep on the blue sofa. I don't think I had done much more than just closed my eyes for a little moment, when you lifted me off the couch and put me to bed. I remember saying 'sorry' when you put the blanket over me and then I fell fast asleep. It was several hours later, when I opened my eyes for a moment and found you sitting on the floor beside my bed still. You were holding my hand looking at me. For two or three hours you had sat next to me on the floor holding my hand while I had been sleeping and when I opened my eyes for that short moment in the middle of the night you saw it and said, 'Look at me, I am on my knees. Don't you see? I love you.' As if you had been waiting all night to throw that sentence in when a gap appeared. At that instant, between sleeping moments, when there is no resistance at all, you threw the message in, and it went straight through all the burning loops to the bottom of my heart without any hindrance.

When you had said what you had waited to say, you left.

I wrote to you the next day. 'Now it's said, there it goes, off it buzzes. In the shape of a fly. Afraid to get lost and later trapped in dark gaping mouths or blind clapping hands. With only one weapon to protect itself: the skeleton on the outside, skin, intestines, heart and soul on the inside. A fly could never be squeezed slightly, it is either perfect or crushed.'

It was perfect, then we were crushed, not it.

5

It was April in Sweden when I returned for my yearly visit. Six months after I saw your face for the last time, in reality. This time I wouldn't really have called it a visit, it was more of a journey to the surface for a fish living in dead water. It was more the hope that a bit of oxygen would be found outside my own element.

I don't know which was the loudest in my sister's garden that month; the sound of buds cracking under the violent hammering of spring, or the creaking of small children's bones eager to evolve.

I had decided I was going to try to catch a big pike before I went back to Africa after a few weeks.

I talked to some people by the lake, they told me that an 8.5-kilo pike had been caught there two weeks earlier and that it had bite marks across the back. So the big one might still be lurking in the shallow waters. There was no time to waste. Especially as I had to catch one for you too.

I have packed away your favourite photograph of me, aged thirteen with the biggest pike I ever caught, nearer five kilos of pride. That one was caught at home. In the picture I am dressed in a blue and white checked dress (changed for the very important occasion. It seems I even brushed my hair for once) and my feet are perfectly together. I am holding out my pike on a big hook to the camera and my smile is proud.

You loved all water, as long as it wasn't dead. (Swimming pools were almost sinful.) Water, salty water especially. But not only because you loved surfing or fishing, you simply loved water.

As far as water was concerned you knew it more intimately than almost all.

As far as water was concerned, it was the only thing you would never have been able to drown in. We spoke of waves and I wrote to you about waves. I said that waves had passed through me too, during those last few days you had been at the coast, even though I was just sitting at my desk in Nairobi. I told you how I found it funny, how some people seem to think that one is more likely to drown in a wave of water, than in any of the other engulfing waves one can suddenly be swept away with.

And that it is a laugh really, how mothers all flock on tropical holiday shores, like pink flamingoes (Spearing the half-shin-height water. Careful, knee-lifting steps on long slender legs, so as not to get *too* wet.), unblinkingly watching their young children laugh and show off their first method of swimming. (Their feet on the sandy bottom but arms pretending to swim). Making sure their little child is not swept away by a nasty wave, foaming at the mouth.

Meanwhile, their husbands, sisters or mothers sit far away from the water, perfectly dry, in the shade with barely a hint of salt-water-air in their noses, waving merrily, still, with heads and lungs full of a wave that makes it difficult to keep their balance (it is difficult to keep your balance when the inner ear is constantly tapped on by a wave). Doggy paddling while eating a cool piece of watermelon, drowning any moment now.

You knew that I saw your fear of drowning in your situation; we didn't speak of it again.

I only told you later that I had a river that ran through my house. It would force its way in just underneath one of the windows in front of my desk and leave by the front door when it rained. And rained it did then, rained, rained, rained and I hardly had any dry clothes any more as only mad dogs and Englishmen stay well covered or inside when it thunders, flashes and pours in Africa.

I told you what I saw when it rained. That there are

people who only see rain as something wet, that makes the flowers grow.

'But you are wet, my dear.' 'No, I am not,' she says quite honestly, counting the drops that fall from her nose to the floor, in a journey from one shape of round to another. 'You see, only a few drops can make you wet,' she says to someone looking at her with bone-dry eyes.

What she knows, you see, is that a raindrop could not possibly be convinced that it is wet. Not to itself! The trick is therefore to deny all alienation from the rain and let wetness become a joke.

You answered that I must watch the raindrops, carefully now as they fell, 'to just pick one, focus on it, watch its thin skin spin, as the sunlight would try to steal it away . . . but no. This one got away, a lucky raindrop that defied those dark gloomy days, when a zillion, billion relatives cascaded down to the earth to be swallowed up by the already saturated soil. No, not this one, this utterly beautiful droplet which had beneath its transparent skin the whole picture, spinning convex reflections, acacias on the upper inner side, all wet and wet, mother cloud below, and onward down as it hastily enjoyed its wingless flight to meet the horizon on your cheekbone . . . where there, really close up now, explosions, tiny tears of joy leaving a cool cool breath, a kiss from the heavens above . . . to you, Anoushka, you who have changed my life, forever and ever, for us . . .'

I sat there in Sweden, at my mother's desk. Bees had appeared from nowhere and I closed the curtains to keep the warm spring sun out while thinking. It was my birthday on the twenty-first. And I took a walk along the beach with my family. I helped my nephew and niece to catch seaflees in kidney-bean-shaped puddles. The water could not have been warmer than fourteen degrees C. I love taking off my shoes, as a matter of fact I dislike wearing shoes all the time and only wear them when I have to. I love sand between my toes, on my skin, in my hair and feel a slight sense of alienation from those who brush it off too vigorously, too meticulously, before putting their socks or shoes on again. When I walked around in those puddles that day I found again a few things I had forgotten for a while, and I discovered that one cannot stop living life to its fullest when one's love is dead, quite the contrary. In the most unexpected places memories lie hidden, waiting to be stumbled upon. On my birthday I found the most delicious present wrapped in a nest of newly defrosted seaweed and seaflees in the Swedish ocean. I remembered the messages you wrote to me in the sand on the Kenyan coast. The messages that you told me only you and the sea would ever know. You phoned me from the coast as I sat at my desk. Many times a day I would pick up the phone and hear your excited voice. Trying to sound louder than the rolling waves or the wind you almost shouted to me that you had written a message for me again. The idea was that you would write a message for me or for us in the sand and then wait for the tide, wait for the sea to eat it before you left. A secret message I would never hear or read, but feel when I swam in any ocean on the globe for the rest of my life.

I look at the contrast of that and where we are now. All the circling hyenas, they count their paintings and lick their chops. The jackals that look for scraps and pieces of bone to steal out of the fire. They want to make flutes with your bones and play their own melody. The smell of singed hair from their paws follows as they skulk off with their loot.

As if you already knew with all the planning of the butcher-shop paintings you were going to do.

For a few more days then I was safe there in Sweden. Fearing the moment I would go back, leave the inside of my Trojan horse of a family. One more time we would go down to the beach for a picnic in the late evening sun. I would take off my shoes and roll up my trousers and see if my tiny godson would want to do the same. My godson I call 'Siagi' for his butter-golden body and voice. I will take his hand in mine, I thought, and perhaps I will see a few of your words here between a child's excited screams at every sight of a shrimp, near white feet turned pink by the still so cold water.

Once or twice as the days were getting longer I have had a moment where I thought that things were getting better, getting brighter, but the anguish is there just under the surface expecting to be brought forward, like a strangling cough waiting for a daringly deep breath to bring it out.

I would be a fool ever to think I could get over the loss of you or compartmentalize it in any way. It would be absurd to think so. The final outcome is far too big to compartmentalize, it is far too monstrous to even bring in through the door to the rest of my life. I turn it this way, I turn it that, I get angry and I beg for help but all is quiet around my heavy parcel, the doorframe, and me. No ship's hold is this big, I know that instinctively. Capsizing threatens at the tiniest bit of weather. I must grind at the devastation, grind it to dust and let a tiny little particle land on each of the cells of my body until it is all evenly divided. It might be that my steps will be heavier from then on, but I will no longer have my vision clouded by obstacles. I despise the bitterness disorientation and darkness bring. The only chance I have must be to try to absorb something that seems too devastating to be part of me. Of course I have no idea of how to do this.

In a room of sweaters and shoes you asked why I was called Anoushka and I answered how it was. That my father had said that his girls must bear names that he could imagine sounding sufficiently beautiful for a man to say when he told us he loved either of us. Perhaps he sat in his work room at home surrounded by egg

39

collections, butterflies and beetles, books and tiger skins, my grandfather's lute and an 'emperor's chair' that had probably never seen an emperor, and tried it out.

So Anoushka it became.

And you said it just as my father had intended.

I must write down the pictures I have of you, of us. It might seem strange but I fear that my emotions may be much stronger than my memory, my heart stronger than my mind, so I have to write them down, so that I may not be crushed under the knowledge thirty years from now that I have forgotten details about you. My memories are what make me strong. Even as I watch the scavengers rip you apart on a bizarre stage with layer upon layers of curtains and flickering backdrops, I can pull away into the shadows and sneak out the back door, knowing that all I wanted from you I will always have with me.

The day before you were killed, you gave me a drawing you had made for me. You took my hand and made it caress the dhow-wood that you had just framed it in. The surface was so smooth that my touch hardly registered when my fingers came across one of the corners. 'This is how the desk will be! The desk I will make you with my own hands. Not a splinter for your sentences to stumble over.'

In return I gave you a word. Of all the words I knew I told you to chose one. A present from my mind, a gap for me And with care you did choose. So a word left me on its last journey from my mind through my mouth. I let it roll over my tongue and take off from my lips and you caught it midair.

And so, as you can never again say that beautiful word, neither can I.

Two hardly used words, exact copies of each other, got up and left.

To think of how many times you hit your head on the beams when you came rushing in, gardenia in your pocket. To think of how small that house was to contain so much.

'I have written something on the back of it,' you said of the drawing you gave me back, and took off in your swirling life.

From the eye of your tornado you brought out stillness for us both. Perhaps if we could have run fast enough, we could have always kept that. But we didn't. We didn't run. In unspoken stubbornness we bent all limbs and locked them. Hooked on to each other's arms and legs, thinking that we could sit this storm out.

6

'Close your hands gently around something you don't know whether to believe or not, and if it exists, darkness is what will reveal it to itself. Like fireflies need full darkness to let them become visible.'

It was in reply to what I had written to you one day.

'I felt sad this afternoon,' I wrote. '. . . Like the day I understood that Father Christmas and God didn't exist, or that the flea circus was not true.' 'A hop,' says the phoney man in front of the children and follows with his eyes a magnificent somersault that one of his trained fleas would make from the palm of one of his hands to the other.

Children – still transparent, definitely, possibly, just a little bit, nearly see the fleas.

I felt sad about the loss of Father Christmas and God, but mostly I felt sad about the loss of the flea show. I had never actually *seen* Father Christmas in his true form, or God, as I thought I had seen the fleas. But my own senses! My senses, that I undoubtedly trusted, I now saw go wobbly at the edges with a frame of mirage. I understood again this day that the world is not round as some so foolishly believe, neither is it flat. I, like Plato, know that it is a cubicle of cubes. Corners and turns can be expected at any moment, and you never know whether in the confusion you are moving or the cubes are turning. What the cube was standing on – the hidden, face-down possibility in your life, just a moment ago – is the reality on top of where you sit and dangle your legs the next.

'Just close your hands gently around anything you don't know whether to believe or not,' you then said, 'if it is true it must reveal itself.'

Fireflies flew out from the back of the drawing you had just given me, when I opened it to look for the message. I read it over and over at a time of this the worst night of my life when it was still not the coldest hour yet and life had fisted its hand around me.

'You'll see, I will be there,' I read.

I did not stumble towards the corner of that road to try and find you. It was dark enough that fireflies lit up my road to unbearable brightness. Fireflies busy stealing the rest of the salt at the corners of my mouth.

I have two mindsets that can be exchanged like keyboards with letters of different languages: the mind of a writer and the mind of a hunter. I have to be in my writer's mind to write. A state where I have no physical fear or pain. The naive luxury of indulging in the human mind. Words pumping through my system like radio waves, where I catch a phrase or two now and again, if I am lucky.

But you brought me straight back to the hunter's mind. Eyes, ears, taste. Legs aching to walk or to stop or not knowing which, but aching. Salt at the corners of my mouth.

Uniformed men stopped me from seeing you then and I hit them, fisted hands inside a fisted hand. Fireflies at the corners of my mouth, stealing the rest of my salt.

Tick, tock, tick, tock and then there are the people who think that time is something that makes things grow, or shrink. But time has nothing to do with most things. A thousand years can not undo the split second it can take for a person to become a murderer, the rest of my life can not undo the few months of love that we had. Time is just a spectator like me. It brings nothing and takes nothing. What makes wounds heal is forgetfulness, not time. If your memory is good enough, time heals no pain and doesn't blur blissful times.

The seed we planted keeps growing and time watches quietly by my side, blinking day and blinking night.

My Rhodesian ridgeback sleeping on my feet seems quite convinced that I won't get up and take off suddenly, like a husk in a storm. I trust her trust in me.

Tick, tock, tick, tock; the only other thing apart from old clocks I know that produces just that sound is the rope hitting against the wood on a flagpole. The rope hitting the white-painted wood in the wind – one of the most reassuring sounds I know. In Swedish summer when days are so long that the nightingales exhibit hubris by so loudly announcing the defeat of darkness. Drunk on daylight, northern shapes dare to live the hours so fullheartedly, to deny that one morning darkness will once again arrive in their bedroom as the first gloomy day of a six-month hangover. What the Lord giveth, He taketh away again. All Swedes know this. When a Swede drinks he drinks enough to make up for an unavoidable hangover that can only be so bad after all.

Tick, tock sounded the rope that hit the flagpole in our garden. As a child I would lie under it and suck in the security that sound produced. And hear the high-pitched shrieks of the swallows. I would lie in the grass with my hands over my face and only make a crack between my fingers big enough to see the golden bulb at the top of the flagpole and the swallows passing over the sky. I would wonder if the Chinese people really ate whole swallows' nests, mud and all, just like that, as they hung under the edge of our roof. And is it true, part-true or just my imagination, that our flagpole broke in two, during a thunderstorm one late summer?

And that my cousin was sleeping in one of the guestrooms when suddenly the top half of the pole came crashing through the window next to his bed? Or did it just almost hit the window? I can't remember, but since then I always wondered what it would be like to wake up so close to the golden bulb that nobody was ever meant to touch.

When thinking back, I always preferred flagpoles to clocks. They are such fools, those who think time has anything to do with anything, or worse, those who say 'don't look at any man now, comparing him with you for all future.' I have found folds of your face in a curtain and walked over imagined traces of your fingers digging up old pieces of elephant bones in the African red soil. How would they understand that?

The other day I was sitting on an aeroplane returning to Nairobi from Sweden. On the other side of the aisle was a crude-looking middle-aged man with a haircut and forearms like a rifleman in the British army. I wanted him to go to sleep as I had already noticed that there was something about his face I recognized. He did. In the middle of some American glossy-ending film, he dozed off, fingers twitching, grasping a great deal, as he fell out of reality. Leaning back from the foldable table, hovering somewhere between vertical and horizontal is where I found the corners of your mouth again. Not the ones you had in the end, but as they were when I first got to know you. I asked you about it later, when your face had changed, had become beautiful, and you blamed it on 'the wires'. We laughed hysterically at the idea of 'the wires' as you called them. All the loose-end, high-current wires swinging freely inside your head like pendulums, until two ends would suddenly collide and light up the darkness with a shock of sick bluish light, casting ugly shadows over your features for a moment. Like a torch held close to your face at an awkward angle. I imagined the wires moving and jolting, a bit like long, frozen pigs bodies, hanging down from big chains on meandering rows of a production line, in a slaughterhouse. Mozart playing in the background, to cheer up the workers.

The humour lived in everything, and the things that we talked about that were not funny could be used in your painting or my writing. Nothing was wasted. It was all used. Looked at, considered and used somehow. We were ridiculously happy and I shouted from a hill over the top of a thousand acacias, just like a Masai warrior with a full stomach.

You hadn't had a rip-and-tear day for a while – a bottle of turps thrown in anger and frustration turning your strokes into multicoloured tears, running down the canvas, before ripping it off. Before strangling what had now become a pathetic clown's face with colours mingling cheaply and with no pride. One big gangbang of colours. Off off, and let in the PH value of air in a wooden frame rather than this hell. I know the feeling. The anger of losing the connection between hand and mind. You said you could sleep well again.

The man on the aeroplane turned his face away in his sleep and I rolled back my eyes to stop the image from being sucked into the ventilation system of the flight cabin.

There I found other images too.

One day you spent half an hour collecting (not picking, but collecting) mulberries from the tree in my garden. You brought them all in and put them on top of my buffalo table. Lined them up with great care next to each other, just to prove to me that there is no one such thing as anything being mulberry-coloured. From white to black, they lay, as placed by your deliberate hands. The berries, quite foreign to Africa, made me think of silks in different colours. Gentle greens, almost white, that smell of perfumed powderpuffs in closed sunny boudoirs. Ochre, soft, like ankle-deep Tanzanian dust that lifts easily around you as you walk, in mockery of all that thrives on water.

'Crystasllitis' was the word you created for the colour of our river. I am sorry to say I still haven't come up with its name, as I promised. You said you had already been all the way down to the river bed. The sand was white down there, the coral reefs were breathing, you said.

That wasn't true of course. We had no clue how things would have been at the bottom, not already.

But you had to be faster than me.

I think you knew what was going to happen. Maybe not all, but something. You feared a disaster.

Or you wouldn't have made me promise to watch over your soul.

I knew only what I felt.

Like the giant insects that sometimes land on my veranda in Tanzania. One kind has feelers longer than its body. His behind is striped in black and bright orange, real orange, like the fruit. I have no idea what place this fellow holds in his world, but occasionally he lands here and strides lazily across my boards. Probably he doesn't even see the nine layers of hills on one side of the house and Mount Meru on the other. With measured slow steps he crosses my veranda, seemingly not worried about anything, yet he is almost all feelers.

7

A few months later I am back in Tanzania. Blessed is the vastness of space around my home.

A Mwarusha[4] girl-child brings the milk every morning, vegetables grow below the foot of my hill. From the village I can hear singing and beating drums occasionally. There are the cockerels of course. But as much as I hate their five-o'clock aubades, at least eggs come from the hens, which honestly is more than I get out of muezzins' calls, should I have been closer to town. I have great respect for Muslims and all that, but eggs would have been closer to my understanding of religion, had I had one. Easter, Jesus, hares and eggs always came together where I came from.

Nevertheless I sometimes have to go down from my

hill. Even if I didn't go on safari, I have to leave my hill from time to time. I might have to go to Arusha to send letters or perhaps to do some shopping. Arusha, a one-horse town of safari people and gemstone miners, Masai and big-bellied traffic police in gloves less white by the hour. The dust going down is so bad that I have to stop my pick-up several times before I reach the main road, just to let it settle enough for me to see half a metre in front of the bonnet. It would be good to have a muzzle like a Russian saiga antelope's here, I think, sneezing behind my rolled-up windows. With their huge nasal machinery, to filter away the dust before the air enters the lungs. But then again, filters in the ears and in the mouth would be a more logical evolutionary choice for my species, for obvious reasons. Road-dust never did anybody much harm.

I went down to Arusha yesterday, to the birthday party of an acquaintance. You would have loved the book I found there. 'Church of Scotland woman's guide. The Kenya settlers' Cookery book and household guide, first published in 1928.' The first page shows one of the uglier pieces of technology the white or brown man brought to Africa.

GCE

ELECTRIC

REFRIGERATOR

a place for everything!

– a pleasure
to own
Delightful
to look at

We would have laughed and widened our eyes in astonishment at the very bizarre and arrogant attitude most
settlers had particularly towards the local languages.
Obviously the memsahibs – as the English women were
known here – used this book, the one I picked up is
in its eleventh edition. Many still have a bit of that attitude. Their great excuse, for not being able to communicate with the locals beyond giving orders, is always
that Swahili is not the language of the locals either.
Swahili is of course just the uniting language of all the
tribes of East Africa (to most their second language).
But very few white people speak any other African
language anyway, so this is a poor excuse.

The only place we ever dared venture together outside
my garden, was a place where we knew no other
Europeans would come. Never around there. Never in
Karen or Langata.[5] The local bar where we met five
different tribes around one table (Wamasai, Wakikuyu,
Waembu, Wakamba and Wazungu[6]). We drank Smirnoff
vodka from little plastic one-portion bags and listened
to Viella who cut the darkness around the table into
smooth slivers with Embu songs that sounded as if they
came stretching from over the same distance as the gaze

of her glazed-over eyes. When she sat down again, she took my hand and put it in yours and said to me that my name in her mind was Nyambura, child of rain. And she saw our love, as did the Masai, the Kikuyu, and the Kamba. Just not the Wazungu. We couldn't tell the Wazungu. You carried me from the table over to the back of your motorbike and we left our secret there with the whole world of the *great Y bar*.

You would have shared my astonishment at how little interest so many people had and still have in this part of the world in talking to Africans. We would imagine red-faced memsahibs on an upward spin in the kitchen, shouting orders in a baby language, with a rancid air of superiority, to people who were even bright enough to understand fragments of sentences with most grammar cut out and pronounced in a distorting accent. I imagine this kind of noise sounded as foreign as the blender to the cook, until he learned 'ki-settler'. (Here they even went so far as to giving this excuse for a language a name: ki-settler! Making clear that settlers were incapable of learning any other language than English.)

To me it is not really the missing grammar or the badly pronounced words, or even the half-sentences that I mind. I still struggle with many parts of the grammar in Swahili, having been here for nine years. It is the lack of interest, lack of humility, the unawareness of the missing words makes my toes curl in my shoes.

The cookbook is of course from a different time. But still I doubt that Europeans in general show much patience and sense of humour to any foreigner working in their country who doesn't speak the official language.

The book would have cracked us up though, like the thought of Sunday walks or words like 'niceties'. And we would have looked at each other with the excitement of being able to see the same images. Feeling rich as our thoughts grew and became one big mound between us. Shimmering under the sun like freshly caught fish, brought in to *one* boat by *two* sets of hands.

'Orders to servants' was the name of this chapter in the book

the divine confusion of:

English	Ki-swahili	Ki-settler
Dust well, do not flick with the duster	Panguse na, kitambaa, usipige *meaning: (Dust (wipe) with a cloth do not flick)*	Piga dusta *meaning: (Flick the duster)*

Wasettler: 'I said PIIIGAAA DUSTAA!!!' Imagine the poor man flicking harder and harder until the heavy frame falls onto the drinks table. Two glasses break and little coasters with horses painted on them scatter on to the floor and Memsahib's shoes.

| Cut the grass | Kate nyasi
(cut the grass) | Kata majani
(cut the leaves) |

Wasettler: 'I say, they are extraordinary aren't they? You ask them to cut the grass and they just attack anything green.'

| Where does the
Bwana sleep? | Hulala wapi
bwana? | Bwana lala
wapi? |

Servant: 'Kumbe, kwa kweli halala wapi bwana??' 'My goodness where indeed does the Bwana (Mr) sleep??'

An insect has eaten this	kimeliwa na dudu	Dudukwisha kula hii
Do you hear? Or listen to me	Kasikia? Nisikelise mimi	Sikia! (add 'sana' *(very)* if emphasis is needed)
Take away the tea things	Ondoe vitu vya chai	Ondoa vitu kwa chai
I do not allow strange boys near the house	siwapi maboi wageni ruhusa ya kuirikaribia nyumba	Dasturi yangu, hapa wageni kuja karibu nyumba
Do not be sulky	Usiwe na ukaidi, or usinune	Usiwe mwenyi hati ya kunune
you are insolent! you must look pleasant, or pleased	Mfidhuli we! imekupasa uso wako uwe wa kupendeza	Wewe jeuri! Sharti wewe tezama chekarea

8

From the top of my hill here in Tanzania it is dry now. It is dry all the way to the end of my vision. It hurts this dryness when goats, sheep and cattle rape whatever little there is still there. And it's only July. There is a long way till November.

Dust-devils whip themselves into frenzy at the speed of their own will and then let go of all they have picked up, become invisible again, pretending not to exist. Warusha and their cattle move past the foot of my hill. They are walking straight into the wind. The dust lies flat and long behind them, like exhaust on a cold winter's day in Europe. It is blackish-grey, this volcanic soil, and it makes the glowing skin of any black man look dry and ageing. Black and white, like a photograph. This soil, that once came from the stomach of the earth, which overflowed from Mount Meru, is the ground upon which I have built my home, or put up my tent rather. The dust gently enforces the understanding that to belong here, is to be part of the mountain. My white bedlinen will change its colour in time and my skin and hair is always covered by the soil of my garden. Dust from the mountain on the palm of my hand lies between me and the touch of my own face. Calmly cocooned in my own solitude I watch the augur buzzard as it lands on the single tree in my view. Occasionally a Mwarusha comes to me, leans on his stick, unblinkingly, for a moment. He will offer many gentle greetings, before saying that he has heard I am a hunter and can I get him lion-fat for his sick wife? Or can he have one of my two dogs?

Empty-handed he will thank me and then start walking down the hill again. Perhaps straight into the wind. Walking with measured steps, on flat feet, like all who are used to hilly country, his red shuka[7] flapping behind him, getting smaller and smaller in the distance until I can only see what looks like a red handkerchief waving in the distance. A red handkerchief waving merrily in the midst of all the eroding slopes.

Erosion is apparent, it always happens where there are people, and it scares me. Strangers' tongues licking your name. Sucking off layer after layer, now that you are no longer here to laugh them away. Trying to decode your ideas and thinking they can interpret who you are.

Layer after layer. As with a gobstopper, they want your name to shift colours, to keep everyone entertained.

Intellectual painter, surfer, vagabond, beautiful, deceiver, murdered, dead, dead, dead.

Slowly getting smaller and more manageable in their minds. They are patient. Their jaws are hurting with your largeness now, but they will suck and lick and crush – waiting for that chewable centre that even the smallest child can handle. That's what they are waiting for my love, to blow bubbles with your centre. But hey Mr Snap, Mr Crackle and Mr Pop, you must have noticed that bubbles of spit just won't make that authentic bang.

Erosion will happen. Here it happened during El Niño. Five inches of rain in less than four hours, was the arm of the bandit that pulled the flush of land, crops and dead animals. Tongues and grooves came undone, and left holes continuously feeding on themselves.

How many thoughts and responses must brush past my own words, how many strangers' glances, over the years, will graze what you gave me, before you change even to my own eyes? I can't stop all the erosion that people or solitude make, not even in my own life. Nobody can. For a while, yes. I longer than most perhaps, because I live a solitary life in a solitary place, but sooner or later it will get hold of you. Erosion takes the shapes of what is already there, then digs and digs, swallowing its own efforts. Writing it down now is the only thing I can do to keep some of it in place, to freeze it as it was.

You sent me so many letters. Some of them are lost. I was too spoilt, far too spoilt. What did letters matter? We had a lifetime in front of us. I was never a hoarder, never a collector. As long as I have my books, some music, my pen and a hunting rifle and I wake up with a beautiful view, you won't hear me complaining.

In my sisters' house in Sweden, I lay awake in a room they had lent to me, thinking about these letters. Did I even read all of them properly?

My mother said, 'Don't worry, my darling. Letters change over the years, you start reading them differently when you get older.'

The ever-changing present will erode reality as it was.

Soon the people whom I meet will look for my past in me, more than I will.

If I get old and toothless, I will look forward to a good mango chutney on my cheese as one of the highlights of my day. Perhaps none of the pain will be seen in my measured cutting of the cheese and none of the loss will be noticed in my spreading of the chutney. My everyday will swing between distracted and content, like most other old bags. Young passionate people will look at my glazed eyes, almost with contempt that the wetness coming out of my body now is just fluids. That the wetness in my eyes or on my lips, is just my body letting go and not a sign of feelings. But just trust me now young friend, it will be there, embedded behind the blue veins of my forehead, behind the jelly of my eyes and jammed up between my gums and my dentures. It is there in the creases of my wrinkled skin, like words on a letter – folded and put away, nevertheless there. Over the years erosion will just make the river deeper, my love, but the stream more difficult to reach. At least that I hope. Anything else would be too dangerous for thinning bones. So let me enjoy my chutney and talk to me about senseless things if that is what I want then. You would forgive me for letting 'us' become part of 'me'. I know you would and they would have to peel me and segment me, like an orange, to get to the pips that will only squeak just before I die, as I too press out the last juice. That way erosion cannot eat 'us' away. Not if they have to peel me and segment me first. Ha!

Right now I am just trying to not turn myself inside out. To keep from eating at my own tail until I have eaten myself up.

9

Let me introduce Anoushka, here she is, fully clad in the isolation she was born with. We are born naked? What a joke!

I have constantly tried to undress ever since I came out of my mother's womb and shall keep doing so. Layer upon layer. Getting and then staying naked is hard work.

So here we go while I remember the truth about how it used to be before you. Let me tell me a story about me. I am a strange person. But you knew that. Or perhaps it is that I just live by my emotions. It could be that what I feel is not so uncommon, but rather that most others let 'events' get in the way. Events that have to be enjoyed at a certain age. Events that really shouldn't go cold while one is waiting and doubting in the queue. They say! And believe you me, that is what they say, well at least that's what they are angling at again and again. Marriage, childbirth and even death should never occur later than *high tide* or things start getting embarrassing. The bridal veil starts looking as if it is hiding something as opposed to protecting her innocence, the child of older parents is expected to be unhealthily intelligent and hushed, a bit like ET. And the old person who didn't depart with the dimming light and elegant fall of the red curtain, leaves a sense of somebody banging into scenery and falling over requisites backstage, while behind what serves as a material wall between the rosy-cheeked death sigh of a maiden at her best age and the reality of empty-eyed memory loss and groping in the dark. They are strict on the loud orchestra at the fall of the curtain, some of those loving families of people who have gone over time. I have seen it. It makes me giggle, somewhere between laughing and crying.

But I don't like events like that, I don't listen to them, they get in the way of life. Champagne should only be drunk, masses of it, when there is absolutely no occasion for it, my grandmother said. Of course I agree. Anything else is a little bit suspicious.

Anoushka was, however, born a loner. When she grew up she met men, had affairs with some. But not a single one of them understood how to live with her.

They didn't understand the difference between alone and lonely. They didn't understand how to never let her feel that her life was cut and fed to the man she was with, for breakfast, lunch and dinner. They didn't understand how she could say that she would never share a home with a man, but longed to share a bed with one she adored. They didn't understand how she could beg for her lover not to go in a shivering voice, pursing her lips like a child, promising anything as long as he stayed for just one more hour. And she would too, have done almost anything at that instant. But then when he had gone, delayed or not, not even bother to answer the first letter he sent to her.

For this they would call her false.

They didn't see 'Hellos' and 'Goodbyes' like her.

Like she saw 'meetings' and 'partings', before she met you that is. But you know about all of that – how she lost her fears of them with you.

To them such greetings were words marking a transition, and they said it as if they were so sure the other always followed one until the end. Like it would never end. Like it would never get quiet, but they could keep on walking in and out of doors for ever.

To her, such words always meant the sudden murder of something that had just been breathing.

She had never understood what it meant to feel lonely. To her being alone meant being by herself. Being alone was being with her self not being without someone else – a natural state of things that she never thought of questioning.

I live on a lonely hill now, this can come as no surprise to you. It was either you or the hill in Tanzania on my own, I could have told you that, but I didn't have to, you knew. But I am talking about before. Before you. Shh wait!

Should someone come to visit her, however, a friend out of the blue, who would come by for a cup of tea or lunch, or a boyfriend who stayed for years, she suffered a thousand deaths in the greetings and farewells. A 'Hello' – however much she might have been looking forward to this visit – it was her world, her reality, being measured, chewed and swallowed by someone else, and afterwards it was that same world spat out, thrown back at her in a confusing jumble of pieces. Afterwards she felt like someone had come into her house, had thrown a huge puzzle of her life onto the floor to amuse himself. They would only ever get a few pieces together and then leave her trying to figure out the rest. When she hadn't been the one to ask for a puzzle.

They would not have been able to understand how she could be shattered, how she could imagine black holes in frozen fear in the farewells of a lover, if she really didn't think much about him before he came or after he left. They wouldn't have believed it and words like false and cold would have been used of her again.

Had they known though, how much true fear, how

much longing, how much passionate love she felt at a lover's goodbye they would have understood. Had they known how much she screamed inside and prayed for a few more minutes, as he was about to walk out the front door, they would have forgiven her, I think! But then I always make the mistake of thinking that anybody would take the time to understand anything or even have the interest. But that is what I tell myself, that they would have forgiven her for even falling asleep calmly and happily with a smooth brow five minutes after he had closed the door behind him.

She understood the idea of a physical lover. Someone who would tell her she was beautiful and touch her without asking or hesitating. Someone who would talk to someone else in a bar and only give her his hand when dressed, but his soul when fucking her in an alleyway a moment later. A bit like docking in space. She hated her lover to kiss her 'Hello' or 'Goodbye'. She wanted nothing from him when he wasn't inside her. Not because she was cold, but because she loved living her life on her own.

But somehow the social exercises, taught to her by the social environment she grew up in, forced her to regard sex and passion as part of a parcel. It was supposed to eventually *lead* to something. An event or other. A few of them preferably. This 'something more important' she could see in the sour glances of some her parents' friends, if she were wearing a provocative dress at a black-tie dinner. Glances saying; the body is eventually going to have to end up as a baby-container. It ought to eventually be a practical household appliance, as, let's say, a fridge.

GCE

ELECTRIC

REFRIGERATOR

a place for everything!

– a pleasure

to own

Delightful

to look at

So what might have started as a passionate love affair, ended as a bunch of promises and demands pushing her on to a floor polished by so many feet before her – like Snow White by the seven dwarfs – to dance the waltz of the fiancée-to-be.

At that stage she would suddenly wake up one night having had the dream again. The nightmare that was about finding herself in a church, halfway up the aisle.

The morning after this dream she would start the slow and painful process of retracting, like an octopus pulling eight arms back into a hole, scraping against the coral in all the hurry.

Or sometimes she would just go, without a day's delay.

*   *   *

Then there were us. Suddenly. It wasn't going to happen. And then it did.

Holding each other tightly when together, letting go completely when apart, but always, always missing each other madly, whether together or not.

'For the first time in my life, I don't feel lonely,' you wrote.

For the first time in her life, she was afraid that she might one day find the feeling he had lost. And she was right. After you died, loneliness picked her up as a long-lost friend and held her tightly, making sure she didn't fall.

Not having known loneliness had been one of her greatest strengths. For this they had called her cold and hard. Later she wondered whether a broken neck is what you need to look warm and soft. Perhaps to some, my head and eyes spinning as if on a thin piece of string, like they did after you left, made me look softer.

But I can't imagine it had much of a pleasing soft-ness to it. If anything, the softness of a drugged person, someone sedated. Nothing closed properly. Her jaw, her eyelids, her hands, her flies, and all the doors in her house, ajar. She sitting motionless for days on end, while bats flew in and out her rooms, in and out of her eyes, without ever touching anything, for it was all ajar. Dogs were barking in the neighbourhood, barking, barking through the night, telling me that I was now, for the first time since I had been born, lonely.

I wake up at night with nowhere to go, no promises to keep and no whispers any more.

10

It is not that I ever stopped dreaming, hoping for impossible things. It would sound better to say that it was something I did only as a child. Imagination and dreaming is forgiven in a child.

When I was quite young, I would write a wish-list several weeks before my birthday each year. I had been told that you could wish for anything you could possibly think of. In my family there was no shame in wishing, like there is in some. To many people in the north, the mere thought of wishing for enormously expensive things would be regarded as presumptuous greed. So I would wish for my own small planet (like that of *Le petit prince*), trunks full of gold and a year's supply of liquorice. Feeling richer for even writing those things down. Feeling rich because mentioning made it a possibility.

I watch the orange and black insect as it takes off from the last floorboard and envy its freedom, it does not regard the air as nothing.

With shiny red shoes that squeaked under the table when rubbed against each other, tight braids and red velvet hairbands, I would sit amongst the grown-ups at the dining-room table on New Year's Eve in the Chinese dining-room. A vividly red room shining in the middle of rooms of pale grey, green and yellow in a dark winter's night. Candles burning throughout the house, fireplaces roaring, the night quiet. Life muffled by snow. I would wonder whether the snow lanterns I had built at the bottom of the garden earlier, out of sight from the kitchen windows, would still be burning like my own shining secret, a kick dealt at the darkness, the great thief of freckles, from me. And I smiled to myself at the thought that they might be burning out there, that for a few hours more, without anybody knowing, I would be culling darkness from afar. And perhaps my mother would be wearing the grey silk dress, the one that gave her wings if she lifted her arms (or is that the one that caught fire, when she got too close to the fireplace, in the yellow drawing-room?). Here I would consider how to get my hand under the table, and then under the dress, then under the white cotton stockings, that made little red stripes on my buttocks and made them itch. Then I would watch the guests, the women and men at the table, and their strongly scented smell would intrigue me. It reminded me of my still so quiet Nivea place on the planet. Like also pubic hair, bitter chocolate and coffee reminded me. And I, like so many before me, would dream that I could fly.

In my imagination I would stand up, and before I knew it, I would start floating upwards, my red shiny shoes dangling at the end of my legs, like plump cherries on a branch. I would just keep going upwards to the ceiling like a helium balloon. That's about the distance I would hover around the world. Ceiling height! I wouldn't let myself go too far up. Not so far that I could not make out people's faces or conversations, if they interested me. Just far enough, that I could turn my back to this world and gaze into another, the world above, where one travels in thinner air and at smaller distances. Just like one of those children's playthings connected to a plug in a bathtub bobbing up and down through the soft line between two elements.

These *still lifes* of my past are all for you. You used to say, you could see them, and I know you could. In return you would give me the beaming, unfolding of your face. You, half-turned away, looking at me over your shoulder saying, 'what I am is all yours when you will have it.' Or else the laughter, from 'inside our droplet' as you called it, the pressing of noses against the transparent wall. Spinning, shining images of reality and two people making faces at the outside world, before the crash and the sucking-up of the soil.

When the belly of darkness rumbles with hunger, I still dream of being able to fly. But now it is more like smoke. A slow burning down to the filter. Perhaps all the way through the filter. I dream that the smoke goes straight upwards when I'm inhaled and exhaled. And whatever holds me alive, I hope to burn its fingers, just at the moment before I am stamped out. That would be grand.

The dreams I have in my sleep are different. Now I dream of bullfights. I often do in spring, when the season is about to start in Spain. I too shall soon be on my way to Madrid to spend a few afternoons in the rising temperature of Las Ventas[8] in late May and early June. But now I dream of bullfighters and arenas full of yellow sand. I dream of muletas, and capotes that are yellow and full of bad luck. And I dream of Joselito el Gallo, killed by a bull, and his opponent Belmonte, and that they married each other's sisters to keep their blood running in somebody's veins. In my dreams it is the only way they can keep the blood running. And I remember that some say that the best bulls cry. There are bullfighters who will swear it. Even in my dream I don't believe it, but I like the idea that they say that it is only the best bulls that cry. And I dream of Belmonte, who was left behind by his competitor, and lost because what quenches the thirst of a Spanish audience is a moment of silence. They tend to love the dead ones more. In my dream I suddenly look at my hands and see that I have no capote. I know that I was supposed to have one. I had one just now and my hands have yellow on them. Colour, from an unlucky capote, that came off on my sweaty hands. And know that I am like Blanque, Joselito's trusted banderillero.[9] And had I been Blanque, I would be in the shadows, pressing against a cool house wall, somewhere away from the people. There are cobbles under my feet and a smell of gardenia, but, it is the essence too long after they have been picked. The smell of brown gardenias sinking into themselves, crumbling inwards with thirst. Folding into themselves with the need for something wet. And I press my hands against the white wall, hoping the lime will come off and hide my yellow palms with white.

They are nightmares, these dreams. I know they are nightmares from the feeling of the dream, but I only succumb to the understanding that they are nightmares, when suddenly I meet your eyes. They are looking at me in the last seconds, as the false yellow sand is growing red under you. Your expression is disbelieving, angry and disappointed. What hurts you is not so much that you are about to go. You have known that was going to happen all your life. The disappointment is at me. At my empty hands. But it is a quiet disappointment, as if I am a child and you know that you had expected too much from me.

'Blanque, where was your capote?' That is what your quiet eyes say to me. 'Where was your capote?'

I look at the false yellow sand, how it sticks in little grooves on the skin on my knees and have no answer.

I wake up. I note how I don't sweat. My body is not trying to get rid of lingering images, not trying to press them out of its system. It swallows it like a horrifying dish of the day. They are the only dreams offered and it is the way to survive. Like hunting a wounded buffalo in Africa. When it charges, wait until it is close enough before you pull the trigger.

Then I lie in the darkness and think of Belmonte, the one who was left behind. When interviewing him after Joselito el Gayallo's death, the Spanish writer Valle Enclan said, 'You have done all except to die in the arena.'

Belmonte answered. 'I am doing my best!'

11

Tanzania is a place where one dances when it rains. At least most do. I can't speak for those who like staying dry. Flying ants steam like hot smoke out of holes at the slightest sign of a downpour and out of joy even buffaloes try to get as many legs as high off the ground for as long as possible.

When I came back from Europe, the first thing I did was to ask the taxi driver about news from Tanzania.

'It has been raining deadly,' was his English answer to my Swahili question, and I thought of how much rain there had been between you and me. A conductor streaming down between our bodies to let us know and hear and feel even when apart.

I love the rain and it was raining madly almost the

whole time I knew you. At least that is how I remember it. It was raining when I lost control, it was raining when you had that first cup of tea on my sofa. It was raining when you rang me from the coast. It was hammering against the corrugated-iron roof, a river streamed in at my desk and left by the front door. You told me you had shouted my name to all the hills riding a motorbike at 140 kilometres an hour on the road from Nairobi to Mombasa. And to me you shouted that you had seen an elephant oddly balanced on top of a rock. I stood in the rain, the heavy African rain that whips anything half-dead into action, and whispered your name, but you didn't hear me. You were far too excited about telling me of all the waves you had met and a new way of riding them. You told me that you loved me, that you could sleep peacefully again for the first time in ages. You spoke so fast.

Margaret and I put buckets under the spouts and filled up the water tanks in less than a day. Now I am looking for desert roses to plant on my hill, to remind myself that some things grow where it is dry. They are sure to survive here. Some things can keep growing when there is no water. Some waves still fold, where there is no salt. And the red irises that grow wild a bit further up, I will plant those here too. I am going to go for a walk up to the spring, where my water comes from, where also buffaloes and elephants drink, that is where I will find them. It will be about a three-hour walk from my hill.

'Stamina is what I have a lot of.' You were wearing one of your very loud shirts. I can't remember whether it was green or orange, but it was one of the two. Your skin was dark brown and seemed still to be covered in salt from your last trip to the coast. 'You will never beat me on stamina,' you provoked me, but charmingly softened my mocking response by kissing my wrists. That's how it was decided. That the first thing we would do when we could finally leave my house together without meeting hatred and cockatrice eyes from those who wanted to part us, was to walk to Lake Natron together. There is no doubt that we were both stubborn. There is no doubt that we both liked a good challenge, and we laughed at the realization that once we started walking neither of us would be the first to ask for a moment's rest.

That year, after you had gone, I didn't celebrate Christmas. Instead I lay hidden under a mosquito net in a hotel room somewhere between Mount Meru and Kilimanjaro, smoking cigarettes. Throughout the night the light in the hundred-watt bulb alternated between brown and white. Relieved when it changed again from brown, to white or total darkness, I found no rest in the Tanzania electricity supply company's brownouts.

Lying there, I heard nauseatingly chirpy Kilimanjaro

climbers coming and going outside my door. Anything I had to give that Christmas was solidly wrapped in cigarette-smoke and whisky, the string around the package chokingly tight. My silent Christmas greetings to anyone passing by my room was:

'Merry Christmas, would you like an implosion? As you might understand it won't explode in your face. No, no it is not an EX-plosion! Don't worry, it won't harm you the slightest. It is an IM-plosion! In the worst case it might steal a bit of oxygen to destroy itself. But it is quite spectacular to see. A bit like watching fireworks in reverse or a perfectly open, expectant flower close its petals one by one, as if it had just been joking before.'

But there are friends out there. In places least expected they step in and take charge. Only friends can see when your legs are about to fold under your body, even though you are still smiling. So a friend knocked on my hotel room door and told me to get ready. Fate would have it that he flew me to Lake Natron in his microlight and nature saved my soul once again. I can swear you were there with me, my love. Perhaps you planned it all that way. The green, pink and white swirls on top of the lake, the thousands of flamingoes flying under us, and their nests that look like strings of mini-volcanoes, made me so much more dizzy with love for life itself than with despair for my own existence.

Nothing can make me feel love like the beauty of nature. If you want to kill me all you have to do is make me look at life from a place where I cannot breathe. Give me office hours, Sunday walks, niceties, tell me that I am not allowed to lie down and fly through the universe with the world on my back whenever I need to, and I will give up. Tell me there are no more buffaloes to hunt and that all my adrenalin has been used up and that I will never be allowed to feel the blood buzzing at my fingertips again, and I will beg with no hesitation. Whisper phrases like 'a comfortable life', 'nice people', and you will see the whites of my eyes growing bigger in the glum lighting.

The other day I heard a BBC programme on the radio. I was outside my tent having a bath in a huge basin, kindly filled with piping-hot water by my helpful Laito. I was pouring big cups over my dusty head and shoulders, watching the heavy clouds between the nine layers of mountains as they did their usual morning slide down to the rift valley, herded by the rising sun. Some psychologist was talking about dreams.

'When we are children,' he said, in his frighteningly charming voice 'we generally have unreasonably high ambitions. When children are asked what they want to be when they grow up, they might say; rock stars, astronauts or the president of America. This is normal. But then we grow up and realize that life is different than we thought and so we adapt our dreams to the reality of our situation. This is important or we might live our lives in constant disappointment . . .'

And so?

I saw words like 'comfort' and 'niceties' float out of the radio. Luckily the wind up here is strong. They blew all the way over to the sliding clouds and by nine o'clock I knew they had evaporated from somewhere at the bottom of the rift valley.

So how do they still the hunger for adventure and ambition that they obviously had as children, all these contented people? I imagine them eating some kind of cement-based pill that will expand in their stomachs to imitate fullness.

> *'. . . Just add water and your stomach will feel full once and for all.*
> *Trust us at WOTALIFE; millions have done it before you and millions will do it after you.*
> *BECAUSE IT WORKS!!!!*
> *Don't worry about the squareness, your stomach is soft and will know how to adapt to all shapes.*
> *Painful indigestion? Never again! At WOTALIFE we say:*
> *What doesn't go in doesn't come out again*
> *Without hunger and craving, no pain*
> *So let WOTALIFE fill that cavity once and for all*
> *TODAY!!*

> If cravings still occur two weeks after WOTALIFE has been taken,
> just keep adding more water until the desired result is obtained.

I have known WOTALIFE people before. (This would have been your favourite part of the book.) They ask acquaintances questions like 'How many potatoes kind of guy are you?' And they would always look at their lover's feet before kissing them – to make sure they are clean.

I remember one evening at the beginning of last October with raw clarity. I hadn't lost my sense of time yet. There is nothing fuzzy about those hours. Each minute measured up to the one before with perfect confidence during that evening. Glowing hours falling off our backs in the night with a clear clinking sound, like crystal glasses purposely smashed onto a marble floor in drunken euphoria.

There were four of us around a table in the little house. A friend had cooked chilli con carne and big spoonfuls of it were dished out into bowls and bread was broken and there was plenty of wine. Knives had no place at this table. Spoons, bowls, and gulps of wine. I sang and I could see that you knew it was for you. You asked me to give you some bread and I took half the loaf, stuck it onto my naked foot and stretched it over to you. Without hesitation you lifted it off, tearing out every crumb my foot had touched, devoured it with a greed that made the rest of us blush and then passed on the one foot-long empty crust with a polite. 'Would you also like some bread?'

I could have pressed your dusty feet against my pounding chest in stolen moments of pause. Crouching, hiding, to catch our breath before our pursuers caught us. The heart needs a moment to build up its full capacity to beat mindlessly, calculated from standstill to tireless galloping there must be catching of breaths to let the heart gain momentum. The step backwards against the trust of all sinew is like an elastic band, that has to be pulled far beyond its natural state, to become its freest self.

Clocks spat on us just then.

12

The last sentence steps into the queue down there, around the corner somewhere. The punctuation mark sucks all my sentences so full of love into its darkness, slinkily, like a string of spaghetti. I can feel how it wants to show itself. How it wants to jump the queue. But I am not going to let that happen. Not yet. I can't let go. Let me bask in the light for a moment for goodness' sake, without constantly feeling that the end will suddenly descend in front of my eyes like a spider on the string it pulls out of its own arse.

Some insane people don't allow for punctuation marks to float for even a moment. They might not allow for them even to exist in their speech. It is difficult to understand what they are saying, of course, but I don't blame them for fearing the punctuation mark, it can be difficult to know what, good or bad, might spring from that burrow as we all stand about it with very little experience. Like the rabbit, that suddenly jumps into the hole, in front of Alice in Wonderland. The rabbit with the watch, again.

No, but not yet at least. *I* decide here.

If I wanted to, I could even become untrue about the whole thing. Why not? Just for a moment. Perhaps what I have written is all fiction. I love you so much, so I can easily write a story based on my worst fears. That's easy. In the evenings perhaps I read all of this to you. Or let's say we invented some of it together, laughing, like we always did, when telling each other absurd stories.

Warm blood, streaming through closed systems in perfect confidence.

At first I was the one to go, but that idea was quickly dismissed. Then it was the both of us. Yes, that is it; we were going to go together. We decided that I didn't try to deny my worst fears at the sound of the shot and that your last shout didn't amputate me, tear me from the pulse. Instead I was so sure that it had nothing to do with you . . . or let's say, I didn't even think before I reacted. So I ran out on the gravel road, and as I turned the corner I just caught a glimpse of your body, fallen. I hadn't even really registered that it was you, before I was cut down by a splitting flash. I never heard the bullet that hit my head. The light travelled at the speed of my final darkness and sound was a foot behind.

But no, that would be too easy. Let's say that we decided finally, settled for the most painful story I could possibly write. We decided that it was just going to be you. I was going to be left behind as the teller, gushing onto the paper what had nowhere else to go any more. Because you had asked me to promise you to do so two days before you left, if ever you should leave before me. We decided this because you are so much more beautiful than me, because the thought of your big sunburned hands frozen somewhere between open and closed in an unfinished gesture, was so much more unbearable than the thought of my far too small and pink hands simply gone limp. I picture us as I imagine we would have decided this, had it been true. We are sitting by the fire, your hair is a bit longer again and you are laughing like the day you discovered the size of my two small fingers. Death is absurd, we point at its ugly face because we feel we can. We don't even knock on wood.

With dread I look around for a gardenia in a small blue and gold glass. There is none. A black beetle, round like a drop of ink, lifts up its patent leather shields and wings thinner than the skin on cooling milk unfold. An unlikely mess of softness about to set sail.

Like the Masai night-guard who used to work for me, some years ago now. I saw his eyes once after you left. This quiet young man, whom I liked so much, I didn't recognize, like I didn't recognize my life any more. I was on my knees in front of him and he went mad for my pain and disappeared into a mental institution in the darkest shades of Africa. All the pride of a crane-limbed Masai gone, locked away behind big pupils and a clenched jaw. Spears and arrows wrenched out of his warriorhood.

I read the letters I still have, again, here on the top of my hill. I am used to this physical condition by now – of sweating when I am freezing. The letters already damaged by some hatred from others are dirty from the dust that tries to cover it all up. The present day is a coward that way, always trying to shift my focus from the glaring reality of my past by covering it in dust or forgetfulness. Nothing a lungful of air still can't sort out though.

And I will keep on reading your letters for however long it pleases me, my love. No matter what WOTALIFE people will tell me is good for me. And WOTALIFE people convinced of the importance of comfort can be almost violent in their approach when expressing their opinion.

'No matter what happens,' you wrote, 'I know that I will always have you to look over my soul, Anoushka who loves me . . . she who sits on my shoulder whispering "I know" . . . smiling with all her heart.'

I will try, my love.

I lie and look at the unforgiving shape of the exclamation mark and can't find the question mark. The exclamation mark that continues to live is the rigor mortis that refuses to let memories go limp and pliable enough to fit something so large. The 'Come in!', 'I am here!', 'The door is open!', 'We are off together!', 'Yours!' are what keep me awake.

A local newspaper prints poor pictures of your face, with a mention of rewards for information. Your body has become a soft handleable question mark. Who? Why? How? This is how some will bury you. How some will decide to fit you in the seven-foot hole dug into the rest of their lives.

That's all I can promise you – to look after your soul in the way that I understand. Your soul in life, not in death. I will turn one of the big blue cups in my hands and drink Tanzanian tea slowly. I will eat mulberries that have no one colour whenever I can. I will let the bees in. And I will smile at the thought of that particular picture you gave me, probably long sold to other people, people lucky enough to have it hanging over their soup, main course and pudding, or their sex lives. I may find a way to see it. I will find myself standing in front of it in somebody's house one day. Nobody will notice when I whisper to us between clenched teeth, while looking at the painting, or perhaps I will wrap a few words around an olive pip and spit it into their garden, hoping that something will sprout. But I wouldn't tell. For, like you, I wouldn't want the 'I' to go away without the 'us' and our love was built on the charm of knowing, not the having.

Even the blue sofa is long gone, and in a year has travelled all the way from Nairobi, Kenya to Dar Es Salaam, in Tanzania, then all the way back to Nairobi where it found a corner in one house, then another. Now I believe it is upcountry on a farm in Kenya somewhere. I imagine that it will be set on fire soon.

There was so much hatred from others around us already before you left. I remember you standing in my little doorway. You had to lower your head to get in. You were angry because of a telephone call from someone who for years had been so good at keeping you ground-bound. You wanted to cry. We looked at each other silently. I could see your fear of looking down and I tried to tell you that you didn't have to just then.

'I don't want the hatred,' I said.

You misunderstood what I meant, and I was caught in that desperate moment of being the only one to know that the words I had sent out had changed on the way to you. There is a brutal instant where you know before you have even half-finished a sentence, that you have been betrayed by your own ability to speak. But it takes a moment for words to travel from one mouth to another's ear. In that moment your face was contorted from the pain of words treacherous to us both. A glimpse of a bitter abandonment. How can one be fast enough now to bring such a sentence to heel before it runs amok, when also breaths have to be taken and new thoughts have to be formed? With a trembling mind I had to wait for my turn to speak again. Damn the time that has to surround a punctuation mark. Damn that black howling pain and misunderstanding that can so snugly nest and grow in the time one has to allow around a punctuation mark.

'Us!' I said, 'Other people's hatred can be around us, but we mustn't let it enter *us*. We must never turn our backs to our past and run. We cannot be built on cowardice. We must soon turn our backs to each other for a few days, only to feel safe from knives until you have dealt with your blows and I have dealt with mine. We will be what we have been built on. We can turn our backs to each other because we will be together. What are a few days, my love? If we run now, how can we not hate our love one day? How can we trust each other?'

In this moment you decided on something. Over your face came a look I could feel in my own stomach. I imagine it was the look I have on my face as a wounded buffalo suddenly runs out from a bush in front of me. You want it, oh yes you want it, but first there is that one involuntary half-step backwards, before you click your feet into the ground. This step doesn't say that you are a coward, it says that you are human, and when you take the next two steps forward you know exactly why.

No, that's wrong, you don't know exactly why, but you have accepted the risks of what you are undoubtedly going to do now. Though a bullfighter trains to move backwards on soft shoes, waving, blinding, confusing, spinning a red cloth, he will undoubtedly stop doing so at the final stage of the third tercio.

The moment of truth had hit us both and so we didn't run away together. In unspoken stubbornness we bent all limbs and locked them. Hooked on to each other's arms and legs, back-to-back, thinking that we could sit this one out.

Mad sundogs in the heat, I never heard them barking.

13

Fervent longing wakes me up in the morning. I sit on my one hill today, looking at nine layers more and ask myself if I should let what I have of you go to the world. If I should be quiet and let them, for some go to great lengths trying to claim you. Yet I don't claim you, I never did.

'For we know, yes we do. And nobody will ever know how much,' you said.

And what else is there? To have is nothing. I don't want to cut a piece of you, to call it mine. All I ever wanted I had for a moment.

I never did see you that night. I did not stumble towards the corner of my road to try to find you, I walked, on dead feet, roots pulled up. It was dark enough that fireflies lit up my road to unbearable brightness. Fireflies busy stealing the rest of the salt at the corners of my mouth. I came up to a uniformed man and a million fireflies lifted me off the ground as the walkie-talkie in his hand said 'white unidentified male shot dead'.

I tried to get through and hit the uniform, fisted hand inside a fisted hand, but was stopped. A million fireflies lifted me off the ground then and carried me the distance a lungful of screams would have carried a body of fifty-seven kilos without dropping it once.

I was never allowed to see your still hands, or touch your hair that even after a cut was so eager to curl again. I was never permitted to go to your funeral. Like a ghost of no rest I circumnavigated the flames that burnt your beautiful being on the Ngong hills. Burned even after your death. Carried to the flames one last time.

It was a soft late afternoon and two kind friends flew me over the pyre, in a small aeroplane.

Twirling upwards with the smoke of your disappearing body like a raptor, my crushed arms stiffly stretched in a cast of metal wings. Only kept up by your rising hot current. Up, up and away. Hard lips open, crying. Calling to get out. Go on, solidify then lips, tap, tap against the air that has become glass. Soaring, now, wickedly replaced by a window-seat, and an engine.

The whole world was on fire that day. Bushfires all around, as we kept flying forward across the acacia plains. They flew me low, smoke, ashes, flamingoes lifting from Lake Magadi.

Do you remember the day you almost ran into my house, as usual you hit your head against one of the beams? You tore open your backpack and produced a painting you had made for me that day. A simple heart on a small canvas, ripped out and onto my kitchen table. Wet, painted half an hour ago, beating. You were laughing loudly, showed me your hands, the inside of your bag, your trousers, my cheek, all covered in paint from that picture.

'Don't you see?' you said. 'Our heart is already on everything. There is nothing I can do.'

By the time I got our painting to my tent in Tanzania, so many friendly hands had touched it, in trying to get it to me from Kenya, that I hardly recognized it. Since, a long time after you had left, it was still wet and changing. Pumping with that same blind refusal of reality, as, on occasion, a shot hare's heart, long after it has been taken out of the warm chest.

Stiff now, shaped into what it will be henceforth, the soothing smell of fresh oil paint slowly evaporating, leaving me helplessly shut out from the process of a thing taking its final form.

Inside my tent, Laito has cleaned with careful motions. I'm just back from a hunting safari and I sit at my desk trying to write my next novel. One of your paintings is upside-down, the painting of the heart that was on everything. Carefully he has taken away the dust that wants to cover it, dust kicked up by the cattle of the Warusha. I imagine how Laito has paused, wondered before he put the painting back. How he must have tried to remember what was up and what was down. It is not carelessness that made him put it upside-down, I know he would have had careful hands. I leave it like that for a moment, it is dry. It will not run or shrink or change now.

In the yellow drawing-room at home there was a particular piece of furniture I spent a great deal of time under as a small child. It was a green, white and pink sofa and had a pattern of chestnut leaves and flowers. In front of it was the insect table my grandfather had made. A big hollow table, its inside clad in white silk and covered by a round glass plate. For hours one could sit and look at all the beetles, moths and butterflies he had collected around the world, when my father was still a small child with big ears and scabby knees. There was the enormous purple and chocolate-mousse-coloured butterfly, the black scorpion, with a stinger bigger than a pea, a furry fat moth that looked like a white owl's face and even a beetle that in my eyes looked like it had the face of a miniature crocodile. All fastened on to the white silk with a pin through the abdomen. On long dark Swedish winter nights my family would sometimes sit in the yellow drawing-room, watching television and I would try to get there before them so I could hide under the sofa. Pinned like one of the beetles in the little space between the bottom of the sofa and the floor I would have to decide which way my feet should turn before sliding in, my head turned outwards, towards the television. I was hoping they would forget about me, so I could stay up longer than expected. Grown-up-time clasped in a dirty mitt with frayed cuticles, caught by me because I was invisible and time was only *almost* invisible.

A tiny chauffeur of time, cruising on forgotten fumes, I thought.

But a moment later, a hand would plummet from above and pull me out of my secret, the beetles in the table were only fixed into the position of looking alive, and oil-paint dries, stiffens for good.

There are never gaps in time, for private ownership. Final form takes its merciless shape. Only erosion after that.

14

'Don't ever let us do something stupid enough to crush what we have. I don't ever want to let greed numb our gentle taste of each other. Taste-buds, so perfect and fresh, should never be pushed into vulgar flowering and sad withering.' For only the eternity-flower does not change if one is not very gentle and careful. On the sandy hills between my maternal grandmother's summer-house and the Baltic Sea in Denmark, grew a small yellow flower we called the eternity-flower.

Whether stretching out its roots trying to catch a bit of the moisture that is always sinking or rising so rapidly through the porous ground, even after picked and squeezed in a small sweaty hand for a while, forgotten for an hour on the sand while the owner of that small hand is swimming, diving, turning underwater somersaults (backwards AND forwards, maximum three in a row) the eternity-flower looks the same. Then sprinting back up on to the dunes and the footpath that runs all the way over the sandy hills, on numb feet and skin that tingles like we were peppermints spat out by the ocean, through the thin line of pine forest that swallows the sound of the sea so greedily and back to the quiet summerhouse of lazy flies and sandy sheets, or not, the eternity-flower looks the same.

Whether made into a wreath and hung on the door that through the years is slammed, closed softly or left to tap gently against the frame when forgotten, it will look the same when we return.

No rotten water in a vase on the bedside table, no falling leaves strewn around, in a last attempt, like most other flowers, to escape from the stench.

A quiet, but intense flower that always looks as if it has just been picked. I have no idea what the Latin name of that flower is, no more than I know the Latin name of the pyjama lily that grows between footsteps of hyenas and duikers on my hill here in Tanzania.

In between laying jellyfish traps for German tourists along the beach and stuffing ourselves with small pink fjord shrimp, any child in my grandmother's house would be asked to go and hunt for eternity-flowers. The summerhouse must have been full of eternity-flowers when my grandmother died.

15

I have malaria. I think I must have that damn thing
again. Could be tick-bite fever; no, definitely malaria.
I want to cry. I always want to cry when my body is
first conquered by malaria. Such a defeat I suppose. I
don't cry with tick-bite fever or any other disease, so it
must be malaria. It comes in waves, especially in the
beginning, before it gets too bad. So far it is not too
bad. I am writhing like a worm on my bed, but not
because I am in excruciating pain. I wouldn't call it
pain, just acute body nausea, limb discomfort. Especially
in the lower back. I know it will go away in a few
moments; I have taken two very large white pills that
are supposed to put the fever down. They will help.

My car has left with a friend and I am in my tent far

away from any decent medicine. At least it seems so very far, now that Laito has left for the village to buy kerosene. Not that I will need it tonight. Unless it gets bad, and in my dream I think that I am awake. That is when it gets scary. My cheeks are burning, like a healthy maiden from the country; they stole the heat from my feet. My feet want to go their own way, yet they are hidden, it is only my face sticking out. The blood is afraid of being too close to any cul-de-sac, but it has misunderstood, there are no dangerous openings anywhere. It is all a fine pressure job under the lid. For three days always exactly at eleven a.m., for some reason, the fever starts. Shuddering, shivering, freezing, burning.

At first I didn't realize it was malaria, I just thought it was from the day I got stuck in an aardvark hole and spent a few hours digging myself out in pouring rain, just to be knocked out by a Tanganyika jack – so ridiculous that there are no words. What an idiot I was to lose my temper that day, I normally know better. The little bastards must have already been starting their strategic plans to conquer my blood then. Patience is always the first thing hoards of malaria parasites succeed in trampling down in me. Well, I was punished for yanking a bit too hard on the lever of a faulty jack. Down came the Land Cruiser, up came the lever, down came I, down poured the rain.

But now it has been three days and I know it is malaria. Tomorrow I have to get a blood-test in town.

I have to get there and get some medicine, I just hope it won't get much worse before then. Of course I am probably wrong. Malaria is a bitch; she never arrives with a polite present for her host. She is a real fucking parasite. The wind has died down for a moment, my tent walls are only slightly vibrating on one side, like jelly, apple jelly. There is a small drawing, one that a Fräulein so-and-so drew for my grandfather. It's a tiger eating . . . something. A sambar perhaps. Looks like they are making love. There is a car, I have to get up. Quick! Suddenly the pace is fast. Good friends visiting. They take me to a hospital. I tell them to go. Blood out of my arm. Wait half an hour on a bed. The lab assistant tells me I must go and see the doctor, he refuses to tell me the result. I hate that. The delay is just to get a consultation fee but it always manages to give you the impression for a second that you have something incurable. The answer is MPS 90 of 200 white blood cells, Plasmodium Falciparum. Malaria! I ring. The doctor says something about women taking over men's jobs. He's laughing. He has a very pink tongue and wears a three-piece suit. Perhaps he was educated in England. He says I must stay. I search for greed in his eyes. I ring. I take Cortexin and Doxycycline. Another friend picks me up and takes me home to his father's house. Think of cool cucumbers and iced water before you throw up in the driveway. Body-ice-earthquake arriving. 'Don't take my clothes off!' Curtains are drawn, doors are closed, the outside closes, blankets and cool sheets.

The fever lies down on top of me.

Sounds like someone is clapping the house wall from the outside. That soft smacking sound confident that nothing will budge. No, it is a skipping rope. It sounds like there is a peacock amongst the playing children, no, have to hear it once more to be quite sure that it wasn't just one of the children shrieking, or a cat. Peacocks sound just like cats sometimes. I remember that from home. Why would there be peacocks? Indians. Standard light blue walls. Somewhere in a hotel in Babati, the big baobab tree on the rusty red road. That kind of blue. Indian washing of all colours on lines. It was a cat. Must have been. A cold hand, then a warm hand on my forehead. The cold hand leaves a temperature mark on the skin of my neck. It stays there.

'You have a custom-made handbag.' Why would a professional hunter say that to me in Arusha? My telephone is on, in my bag, somehow. I can hear an angry woman's voice hissing at me from far away. She continues. It sounds crisp and razor-sharp. It makes me nauseous. But there are only five holes in the phone for the sound to come out of. Thank God the zip of my bag is closed. The zip of my tent, but not my tent on the hill. I am in a hunting camp. I am asleep.

I heard your voice outside the tent. You said you wanted to go down to take a bath in the river. My lips are dry, my tongue feels swollen like a cork in a bottle. The place where I used to enter the river is not very far from my tent, perhaps forty metres away. A few steps down the steep bank and you would be able to walk out onto the big rocks that formed a pool in the middle of the river. Flowing water passes in through a small chink in the chain that parts me from hippos and crocodiles, and water flowing out again on the opposite side. I can feel the quiet presence of you in the tent, but don't open my eyes. You must have come in to pick up a kikoy[10]. It is getting dark outside. I know it instinctively. It is getting dark, my love, be quick. Come back soon. There are tsetse flies in the room. They bite. Fill their black bellies with my blood and feed it to their children. We all eat each other – the horror of that. The photographs you showed me for some of the paintings you were planning to do, flash at me, even your own image was mirrored in Kenyan butcher-shop windows. Half-cows, whole goats on display. Dark red meat and yellow fat swinging on hooks behind crystal-clean windows, attract passers-by. Metal shutters painted with dead meat images and words. *CHAPS, HIND QUARTER, FLY NA, TAKE AWAY*. The horror-humour in that. You roared with laughter.

There is a pause.

I must have been gone for a long time. Perhaps. It is so cold now. Where are you? I am hot. It is all so quiet. Why is it so quiet? I haven't heard any voices for a long time. You went swimming. It is a long time ago.

Something has happened. I just know it. I know it. There are crocodiles and hippos. I must go there, to the river. But I can't, I can't get up. I can't get past the fallen flagpole outside the tent. Even if nothing has happened, I have to warn you of all the crocodiles they come out of nowhere. I have to run. I see frothing water, waves foaming at the mouth. Eyes too open with fear and anger of losing life. I know it but I can't get up. The golden bulb that one is perhaps never really supposed to ever be so near, is blinding me.

I wake up wet with sweat. There are lines of light coming in between closed curtains and low voices from the veranda outside. Calm voices. The African day would start burning soon enough. Gentle scents brought out by the night would soon close up and give way to the smells and the rot that belongs to the sun. I am in Arusha after all. In a strange house. In a strange bedroom, with unfamiliar smells and dark sheets. A dog barks again and again and the sound is maddening like hard rain on a tin roof that never seems to want to stop. It is comfortable if for a moment, reminding one of normal life and security, but maddening if for long, reminding one of normal life and security. I don't want to rush the thought process as it uncurls and slowly rises above feverish confusion and nightmares. I don't want to hasten the lifting of the mist to face steadfast mountains still only sensed in the white oblivion. There is a moment's relief, an instant of true happiness as I realize that there are no crocodiles near, that you are safe from them. I smile at that thought, because the truth, so near, could still be anything, could still take any random path. But the mind will not rest here. It ticks away like a machine trying to break a code to a bank box. It will not give up until the numbers click into place and stop. And then comes the answer! Bingo. The golden code that opens all doors to my past and present has arrived to shine firmly out of the whites of my eyes again. The reality of you hits me in the glabella, with the ricochet of my own thoughts. An innocent question, thrown against a mountain, caught and thrown back at me dumbly by a mountain wall turning into a rising troll. Lasting silence roars a perverted song, like a lonely drunkard waking up dogs and sleeping people.

The hoarse voice of silence. I lay back on my wet pillow for a moment longer. I remember one shape of silence that met me before I could have understood its kind.

When I was at the age where I would smile with my mouth closed, because my teeth were all new and too big for my small head, and my shadow had a hard time following my scabby-kneed scissor-legs in the pale Swedish days, I met the idea of silence in a way that would take me many years to understand.

As a child my sense of boredom on dead-weather

days would only ever go so far. When I got tired of drawing, I might go on a route through the house.

I would caress the narwhal's long twisted ivory tusk that leaned against the hall stairs, imagining its lonely journey in deep oceans.

Take a peak at the egg collection of birds from all over the world if my father or the secretary wasn't in the office.

Perhaps lift the lid of the silver pheasant to see if there was a sweet I could take without being seen.

Or I would be in a far-end corner of the house, watching fat bottle-flies caught in between double-glazed windows, whilst enticing the snow to begin falling with home-made songs of a pathetic nature, so pathetic in fact, that I recall a few tears rising out of self-pity for the grand words I was offering the heavens above.

(The self-pity of a child! Melancholy is something we in Sweden only understand later. The dead of winter oozing in through the windows is not noted until grown-up dread of darkness has taken the place of childish joy for snow. When we no longer sing the song of the first snowflake, stumbling over our little heavy boots with excitement to get out and throw the first snowball of the year. *Ja se det snöar, ja se det snöar det var väl rolikt hurra!*[11] I fled the north before I stopped singing the snow song. But the melancholy of spring had caught me earlier. When I had only just passed my childhood years, its arrival used to make me so happy that my heart could not help but swell with shy melancholy for the many months I had longed for it so openly. Like a loved one, just returned from a long journey. A moment, spoken about so often, longed for so deeply, that one cannot bring oneself to embrace it.)

As luck would have it, normally I wouldn't be found in the house, but would be left alone to nourish the budding understanding that springs from childhood loitering. I had just learned to read and words were filling enough in their singular sense. Sentences, especially ones that had to be consumed (sentences that one has to bounce against the inside of one's mind to hear the echo that brings out the meaning), I didn't see yet. Sometimes I would sit in a chair in front of rows of books trying to read some of the titles. I still remember two titles. Somehow they made an impression on me and after reading them the first time, they would catch my eye whenever I walked past. I never took either of the two books off the shelf; I just sat at a distance and spelled my way through the words. The one made an impression on me because it was in a foreign language and the words sounded adventurously far away, the other because I sensed that there was a deeper meaning behind the words, incomprehensible to me. I never knew then that I would ever understand the deeper meaning of course. The world was full of incomprehensible things and I accepted my ignorance with the same open-faced appetite as the plate,

111

miraculously put in front of my nose three times a day. (I still don't really understand what it is fair to expect from my own understanding of life, or even of life itself. I have no sense of fairness or unfairness of the portion on my plate. I just lift the fork, and ask for more if there is more. What else can someone hungry do?) The one title was *Nuns and Soldiers* (noons aund sooldeeirs to my Scandinavian tongue); *Tilsidst taler tavsheden* was the Danish title of the other book.

When my mother left our home (I now suddenly remember that we had a birdcage made of porcelain in the yellow drawing-room. Did she leave the door of it open on purpose when she left, or was that a coincidence?) and moved to Copenhagen in the beginning of my teens, she took the two books with her. I followed her a year later. Again, I never thought of taking the books off the shelves. I just noticed those two titles and wondered about them every so often. Now with the gaze of a teenager, suffering from my first hangover, or my first boy trouble.

When I went back to Scandinavia last time, now certifiably a grown-up, my mother had left Copenhagen and moved into the old gardener's house on my sisters, property, in southern Sweden. Walking across frosty grass I entered her little house. The moment I opened the door, orange warmth welcomed me back to the inside of the Trojan horse from where I had sprung. A traditional Swedish Kakelugn[12] blazing in each of the rooms of the little Carl Larsson[13] like cottage, was a mother's way of making sure that what was soft in my soul didn't freeze up, if she could help it.

Her boxes of books had not been unpacked and I offered to put them up for her. As they passed through my hands and on to her shelves one by one, I eventually arrived at the two books with the familiar titles. Oh, I thought with a smile, it's Iris Murdoch who wrote *Nuns and Soldiers*. At least I knew the author by now, even though I had still never read that particular book of hers.

As for *Tilsidst taler tavsheden*, I picked it up gently, pleased to finally get a look at what this strange title would offer me now as a thirty-one-year-old woman. My heart stopped for a moment when I saw who the author was.

The words of your mother, my love, had been there always. Quietly collecting dust, waiting for me to pick it up, when the right time came, and so I did. For the first time, six months after you left, her title 'Silence will speak' made perfect sense to my ever-changing understanding of life.

And so silence does. Shouts rather.

A sounder sleep later, I slowly I sit up in the bed of the kind soul who nursed me back from malaria fevers, and look to pick up life where I left it.

I drive back to my hill, past cows and goats and young Warusha boys wearing black, their painted faces framed by long ostrich feathers. The pyjama lilies nod their heavy heads beside my car going up the hill. Sixteen lilies on one stem. I feel right here. In front of me is what the Masai call the Mountain of God, Oldonyo Lengai, and the deeper than the ocean rift that runs through Africa, the world's longest scar, approximately six and a half thousand kilometres, stretching from Palestine to the Beria coast of Mozambique. The sun as I meet it rises just to the side of Mount Meru and sets just slightly to the side of the Mountain of God and the rift that cuts into the marrow of Africa. A young Mwarusha girl brings me milk from her father's cows in a Konyagi bottle, that he no doubt emptied of the local white spirit one night. She bends her knees slightly and holds the bottle with both hands as she gives it to Laito, her black eyes nowhere to be seen. She waits for him as he pours it into a pot in the kitchen-tent, and since he is not there she lifts her head. I am in my bed and don't see her, but I know, I have seen her often. She wears beads of all colours around her wrists, around the ankles of her naked feet and she is in love.

The wind is blowing again, the day, like the year, is coming to an end. The sound of drums, hyenas and chanting warriors from the village below just slips in beside me as my lids close shut behind us. I fall out of reality, wishing you were here to close your hands gently around my doubt. I know I would then try to shine like a firefly in the darkness, in my thirst for light. Like most living things.

16

When I wake up I feel stronger again. There is a letter next to my bed. I'm invited to attend a ceremony for young warriors-to-be, later that day.

A flock of guinea fowl scuttles off to a cloud that is still resting on my hill and I imagine them taking off together, the birds flying freely in white oblivion for as long as they want. And then when they are ready they drop out of the drifting cloud, and from a distance it looks like the sky is raining rocks. The whiteness they leave behind is only a dead skin thrown off, never to be seen again. They can choose when to fly, when to leave the cloud. This is bliss as I imagine it. But I was born without eyelids. Life force-feeds me like a prize-winning goose, there is good and bad in that.

As I go outside my tent an augur buzzard takes off from its resting place on the railing of my veranda. The ceremony is today. I can hear them coming, before I see them. And then, a couple of hundred metres away, at the foot of my hill, they pass. A few dozen young men about to be initiated into the Morani-hood of their lives, a decade or so spent as warriors to prove their worth and pride as Warusha males. Off on foot to a big boma[14] of one of the elders, they carry the flag of their area and are followed by all the eligible young girls that they claim belong to their blood. Here they will meet up with other clans, and hundreds of new Moranis are born on this big day. The proud flagbearer runs up and down the two marching lines to show the whole world their heritage. Their faces and bodies are painted in red patterns and they wear ostrich feathers, lion and colobus monkey skins as magnificent high headgear. Their hair is long and as they walk, heavy bells tied on to their thighs jingle dully to the accompaniment of high-pitched war cries and the trumpeting on several greater kudu horns. Lobulu my nightwatchman is there and even though it begins to rain heavily just when he sees me coming down the hill, he stops and, face beaming, asks me to take a photograph.

'Are you soaked?' I asked on the telephone one day. It was raining so frantically that I had to shout over the noise of cascading water drumming against my tin roof.

'I am ashamed that I am not,' you answered. I revelled in that you understood what I meant.

'Only mad Englishmen and dogs won't go out and get soaked under the torrential rains of East Africa.'

'Why didn't I go out? I don't know. I meant to . . .'

'Hmm, this is not good. Bisto (your word for WOTALIFE) . . .'

'Perhaps Bisto is contagious. There is so much of it around here. I tried to paint today. Total disaster, mind-fuck – in a way that you would understand – welcome to the Barbara Cartland club. As you are a writer they will give you a life contract with Mills and Boon . . . yup, that's it. We could throw all that Bisto lot into a giant vat together, blend them all and create a lethal concoction to numb the brain forever. Now that I have perfected my photo-real technique, I could lead the crew for that good old honest "I like to see the things the way they are" club . . . and stop trying to show them abstract painting. I mean who needs to know what that damn cat looks like, acatisacatisacatisacat! I will see you later. Anoushka I love you. I love you Anoushka. Anoushka I love you. I will see you later.'

Twenty minutes later you were there. Gardenia intact pulled out from the inner pocket of your jacket. The white softness of the flower in your hands.

'I thought of cutting a finger off, to give it to you. What else can I do to really make you understand?'

'I understand.'

'Perhaps you don't! Perhaps you will only really understand if I give you my flesh, bit by bit. Words can only take meaning to a certain point. The horror of word poverty, of speech and lovemaking not being filling enough in the greed for each other. Do you see the headline? Two lovers found dead and half-eaten . . . by each other.'

We had tea on the blue sofa and you spoke of bones: elephant bones for the tables you made, giraffe bones, the little edge of bone that sticks out on top of a shoulder, and I kissed you on that soft spot between the jawbone and the ear that is so easily forgotten otherwise.

After walking for about one hour we arrive at the boma of their destination. The young girls, who walk separately, behind the men, have shaven heads, kilos of bead jewellery around their necks, foreheads, ankles and arms and blue material wrapped around their bodies like long togas. Today they will flirt ruthlessly with the warrior of their choice. There is rivalry and they can be as bitchy as any women around the world, perhaps even more openly than most. They sing the sweetest songs with honey voices yet one warrior is constantly with them to make sure they don't fight and rip each other's favourite jewellery to pieces.

There must be more than half a thousand warriors, elders and young girls when we arrive. And me – a face with nothing better to do than to bob its whiteness in a sea of black splendour. An old toothless lady, with earlobes so long that they touch the jewellery around her neck, lifts up my hand in hers above our heads and emits a war cry. I am quiet and feel welcome but slightly out of place. Children don't dare go near me, but flock at a distance and I tease them by suddenly taking a step in their direction when least expected. They scatter, like a handful of marbles dropped onto a stone floor. The smallest ones shriek, their eyes fill up with tears, they horror-laugh and run to hide behind their bigger sisters, who stand still, at a safe distance. During the whole ceremony, I hear a constant whisper hip-height. Little voices that get sucked into the noise of war cries and mock fights and evaporate, like tiny raindrops on hot ground.

'Mzungu, mzungu. Angalia! Mzungu.'[15]

They come to the bull slaughtered in sacrifice, its black hide is stretched out on pegs. They dance around it and finally charge, clashing each other's rungus[16] above it – an action saying that they have now entered the Morani-hood of their lives. High on an infusion made from the bark and root of the Acacia Nilotica, some of them eventually start frothing at the mouth and pass out in mori, cramps that make their bodies stiff like planks. One has his arms stretched out above his head so stubbornly that thrice they come flying up again when gently bent down by the three men who have come to carry him away to rest. 'A drug that will make the happiness rise from your chest until it reaches your head,' Lobulu told me before he passed out in mori.

I arrive at my hill again, just before the sun sets. I stand on my veranda with my dogs and a whisky feeling more grateful than ever for all that I have. Empty-handed wealth, wrapped up in the peace of a moment past, eyes caressed. This is an experience that will be with me now, in my bones, a spreading secret that cannot escape or even really be told.

17

For thousands of years there has been a quiet understanding between a clever little bird in Africa, called a
honey guide, and humans. It is quite true that if you
follow this plain-looking and very noisy creature, it will
lead you to the honey it has found, but cannot get to
without help. Flying from tree to tree in front of you,
it will take you to the treasure – the unspoken agree-
ment being that you will take part of the honey and
leave some for the bird.

Of course there is no knowing how far away the
honey is, or how difficult it is to get there. A bird does
not care, it flies. Sometimes it even seems that it gets
itself lost, but that might just be at times when I lost
faith before the bird.

Anyhow – there is a story about this creature. A myth. It is said that if you eat all of the honey and leave nothing for the bird, it will lead you to danger, next time you chance to meet in the bush. It might sing so alluringly that what you hear is a promise of a tree-trunk full of honey. While you are blinded by the desire for the sweetness that awaits, the bird will get you helplessly lost or make you run straight into a hungry lion that will eat you or an angry buffalo or elephant that will kill you.

With enough patience and water nobody can ever be lost of course. You were not lost.

A single bullet to your heart killed you, killed on the way to me. I was expecting you. There were just a few steps to go. My gates had already been opened.

There was so much honey, my love, and we took it all. You know we did. We ate it because we had found it in a place that nobody knew about. But we forgot about the honey guide of life. The greed we had sworn not to have about each other we didn't have. Instead we were greedy about us, foolishly thinking that that is not the greatest greed of all, greater than the greed for each other.

My mind that an instant earlier had frozen and turned to brittle ice by the sound of your shout, was shattered by the blow of a single shot.

Blinded by a million fireflies, I grappled for any truth but the truth.

Deaf from the sound of sudden silence.

The single roar of your anger, surprise, fear and then the shot that appeared from nowhere, throwing its poison at me and then, like a spitting cobra. slithered away into the tall grass, to leave its victim's eyes full of blinding venom. So I tried to catch the serpent, but the serpent was laughing, was just a tail with no body, no body to be caught. A job well done in a serpent's world. Now my blood would carry the truth to my heart and I felt the world turning like the cube Plato says it is. The lucky number that had been about to appear on a couple of dice, breaths held, excitement quivering, as one dice stood on edge. The faith so perfectly strong. Winners or losers-to-be, begging for a five and a six. All lost in an instant.

Sanity took off and all shooting stars from my thirty years on this planet reversed to their previous places on the sky. Sat unquivering, unwavering.

Your shout, my love, crushed me. Took hold of the loose end and with one yank unravelled my all. The sudden darkness of a true African sunset.

Twenty minutes is all East Africa will allow your eyes to get used to darkness at the end of every day. Only twenty minutes to prepare for a moonless night. But it takes so much more time for the human eye to reach full capacity to see in the dark.

In that moment of time, the inner eye speaks, the ears see just enough to part ceiling from floor, and the soul whispers for the mouth to be still. Trust is the only sword to make heads of cunning demons roll then.

And that is where they live the demons, all of them, In the moment between sunset and night-vision.

18

Faced by a lion, the last thing you should do is to run. If it does not have the intention of pulling you down as you happen to stumble upon it in the bush, it might be tempted to do so if you turn your back and run off in a scrambling panic. It is tempting, for all creatures, again and again, to do something that they are good at. And they might.

'Do you know? It is the most extraordinary thing . . .' I said to you on the morning of the last day. '. . . the tree outside the kitchen window . . . I suddenly see that it looks like "The Scream" by Edvard Munch.' I had no fear in saying this, I was talking to a painter. We laughed.

Now I let the sound of your last shout be absorbed, slowly, into my bones, as the only way to survive without losing my mind. The bones are porous like the volcanic soil of my garden, but the mind is not. The bones that carry soft flesh and skin have a core to be filled with a lifetime's worth of honey and spilled milk. There is no point in trying to deny the sound, it sits in my ears like the sea in a conch. I have to let it play again and again until the numbness of habit turns down the volume. To turn my back and run would be the worst thing I could do.

It is all a matter of trust. We walk so calmly on the ground, trusting our feet to carry us the way we choose. We don't expect to stumble or slip on a dry pavement even though it might not be as broad as we would like. And yet take that width and lift it over a gorge and ask us to walk over it, and we might fall into the abyss in sheer fright. Over a gorge, sanity and trust in our ability to stay on the plank come at a price.

I don't have any eyelids and don't turn my eyes upwards expecting to find any answers there. I look down into the horror, such is my nature, and your last shout comes at me. I see it, I hear it again and again, but there is nothing I can do but to put one foot in front of the other and hope to get used to it eventually. I have been gun-less and on foot in front of lions before. It is difficult to know what is going to happen, but I know what not to do to give myself the best chances.

In times when the instant reflex to a severe situation

needs to be snapped at the neck, there is always a moment of choice. Picasso said if you want to paint a table, paint a chair. When I want to run, I stand still or sit down for a moment, this is my way of running slowly. It is not about courage, it is about fear, fear of stumbling in the gap between sunset and night-vision. The moment of choice can be helplessly short, but it might just decide the rest, like the most inconspicuous comma in a sentence.

That's why, after you left, I was careful with the keys. The keys around my neck that open and close doors like magic, as if I have nothing to do with them, were suddenly in front of me. The string they hung on had been caught in the tangle of the shot and your last shout and yanked them off my neck as I fell onto my hands and knees. With open doors, restless keys will only do one thing. And if locked doors cannot protect you, there is no point in them any more. So I threw away the keys and left everything open. I broke the glass to the clock and pulled its hands off. Tick tock away. What is it that tries to fly away, but never gets to the door? Time! Now what can it do? If you break the hands of time, a moment is an entity in itself not a lifetime divided by a thousand.

I never considered leaving Africa after you left, I have had so much stolen here so how could I leave? Locked doors do nothing to thieves in the night if they really want to get in. Radios, watches, fountain pens, money, a computer, whisky, clothes, even hunting boots. Before you know it Africa has stolen your heart too and carved its name into your soul. It is normal here. A day comes then, when you can no longer see what is Africans' and what is yours. So I stayed of course, knocked in the tent pegs with greater conviction than ever. Became yet another white dog of Africa – the more loyal to my master for the kicks in the ribs. Vaguely aware of owing or being owed something, aware that here is debt but not what the score is. Africa has already taken so much out of my hands that I am more ready than ever to adore her when she opens up and unfolds her beauty.

And when she does do that, no other place I have even seen has quite that hand of feeding me, scraping my chin with the spoon and wiping my mouth.

And all I can ever do in my inability to communicate with her is to open my mouth wider, whether it is food coming in or a shout coming out.

I don't know any more if my stomach is swelling with fullness or with hunger.

19

I took a buffalo-hunting safari the other day, quite a bit south of my hill. The camp I was staying in was just by a river. Hippos kept me awake at night, insisting on chewing grass very loudly just a couple of steps from my bed. I had to cover my head with two pillows to be able to sleep. There were two beds in my tent. I lay in one and a rifle lay on the other. Just like it used to be when I first arrived in Tanzania almost nine years ago. Bliss that; to be dog-tired and fall asleep to the sound of roaring lions, knowing that tomorrow, if you are lucky, the bush will offer you that motivation that only the tantalising pursuit of a fresh buffalo track can evoke. Yes, come back please, the buzzing at the fingertips, aching legs, aching from wanting to walk or wanting to pause for a moment, where the want will be stronger than the body and I don't exist beyond my own senses. Pausing, then cut the tangle of roots off and just take in, suck in what juices is bid my clear severed stem, with the pure force of nature. Because I can't help it. And blame it on that too: that I am alive, sucking life, because I can't help it. My whole being fitted back into place, inside the mould that I came from. I am incessantly surprised, that it fits so well.

The joy of being awake in the early mornings, when most are asleep: about to set out on a search for a track, a scent, when all in the darkness seems calmer than one's own desires: desires, sleepy and still warm from being close to dreams interrupted, and known rather than felt at this hour. I get to the mess before anybody else, except for a kind soul who has put tea on the table, lit two kerosene lamps and left. Then slowly, at the speed of hot tea in small gulps and the quiet sound of a hunting car pulling up beside the mess, I'd cool from the moulding of sleep and become finished stature with dawn. Stars fade, darkness slides off the sky as a blanket kicked off by waking limbs in the rising heat. Suddenly, from darkness to bright day, for a few hours all is more intense and awake than it will ever be, when hopes are high for a hunter and all living creatures move with the confidence of a rising day.

Hunting is what brought me to Africa, it's as simple as that. To hunt buffaloes is why I set foot on this continent. Food, lodging and one buffalo was the deal I had with a professional hunter as my payment for my first year's work as his apprentice in North-western Tanzania. I still love them, the buffaloes. In their massive black stature lies the possibility of an adventure that might creep up behind you before you can creep up on the buffalo. Their stiff-legged gait is in my grandfather's turn of a pen, in tales from encounters with dangerous game around the world, in the 1930s. Their muffled, lazy talk in the late afternoon, as they begin moving towards water, is my grandmother's whispers to a small northern child, with pupils the size of large peas, before bedtime. For me, to sit on an anthill island and watch them walk past, with adrenalin pumping comfortably, fingertips buzzing with thick blood. Their smell is enough. One stops, stands still for a moment, you watch its frozen profile as it listens intently. It tosses its head and it might as well be towards the slight sense it has of you so near, as towards a bothersome fly.

The Tanzanian hunting season is over for this year. But I will go back next season, when it starts again. I will try again. I will because I can't help it. Perhaps I ride on the back of life like the scorpion the frogs carried across the river but I will squeeze the orange until the pips squeak. We were, we are, the same in that respect.

Behind layers of walls, mosquito netting and the noise of people graffiti-spraying syllables at each other, I tend to lose my vision of the wholesome reality of hunting and being in the bush. But when I come back I exhale, I exhale dead air.

'I have thought about it,' you wrote, 'as you have, your already broken body tossed in the air by one of your friends . . . I know that it is a possibility, but it is clean, instant. And part of the deal, the excitement for you, is that very possibility . . . Now those are the Sunday afternoon walks I'll do any day.'

I don't think I answered that letter of yours. Not because I found it frightening or disturbing, but because the thought of me spinning to death on a buffalo's horn already had found its fuzzy place in my shadow. Like all hunters still hunting here. Shadows only ever grow in jealousy of a growing sun. The reality of my own end, like a small gnashing dog perhaps, nipping at my heels as I walk, is never taken more seriously than that. I see it as it follows, I have got used to it, it seems quite harmless. Short little legs.

One's own death is just a pet, until, drunk on life or simply by stumbling, there is a fall, then suddenly anyone can be had by the throat. They say that even a poodle has the soul of a wolf.

But on the other side of life, pressing enormous and heavy against the door that divides us, is real death.

The ludicrous keyhole vision we have of death!

Here, from the side of life, we try to have a closer look at death through the keyhole in the dividing door.

The keyhole-shaped fragment of death, the mere detail of this much larger shape that happens to be pressing against the hole in a particular moment and time is what we can see, and this vision leaves us no closer to seeing any relevant form.

Death is too close.

Cubistic, living thoughts of death: a moth, eight-thirty in the morning of a brand new day, its wings glued to the milk, or one's own life looked at with a pair of binoculars turned the wrong way, cannot possibly bring us nearer to the understanding of death.

Death is by, and more familiar smelling to anybody's nose, than the armpit of our own mother, as she reaches over our shoulder to put the milk on the table. A smell we have known since the day we were born and therefore cannot possibly single out from the smell of life.

Familiarly-near, silver-dust-on-your-cornflakes-near, laughably-near. Ha ha! The day you stood under the mulberry tree, gently breaking off all small twigs at the height of my eyes and talked of what you wanted should you die, I recorded it with interest, not with fear. You didn't say it with fear.

The sun, shining through the foliage onto your face, made patterns of light and darkness, mysterious and gentle for us.

No different from the image of two lovers madly and secretly in love, talking of death.

NOTES

1. A duka is Swahili for a shop.
2. Kamba. A tribe in Kenya.
3. Karin Boye (För trädets skull 1935)
4. A Mwarusha girl is a member of the Warusha tribe. The Warusha are related to the Masai. There are a number of differences between the two tribes. I am sure many experts have an idea of where those differences lie exactly, but I chose to stick my head through my tent door and ask my Mwarusha nightwatchman for his take on the matter. His answer was that the Masai are more nomadic and don't farm the land, that the languages are slightly different, that the Warusha don't remove one front bottom tooth like the Masai and that the Masai sing for three days before getting circumcized (the Warusha one day). Finally he told me with a very loud snort that the male Masai go home and stay with their mothers for a couple of months after

they have been circumcized and that the Warusha would never think of doing that.

5 Karen and Langata suburbs of Nairobi, where most European settlers in Kenya live.

6 Wuzungu is plural for European.

7 A shuka is a red (often checkered with a little a bit of blue and or yellow and green woven into the pattern) blanket worn by the male members of Masai or other tribes related to the Masai, like the Warusha.

8 Las Ventas is the bullfighting ring of Madrid.

9 Banderillero: a bullfighter's assistant who handles the banderillas (darts stuck into the bull in the second of the three parts of a bullfight) and also protects the bullfighter from being gored where the situation permits using his capote (a bigger and stiffer cape than the one the bullfighter uses).

10 Kikoy is a piece of cloth, traditionally worn in Kenya by men.

11 Swedish children's song: *There we are it's snowing, there we are it's snowing, what fun that is, hurray!*

12 A *Kakelugn* is a traditional Northern closed fireplace.

13 Carl Larsson was a Swedish painter.

14 A boma is a kraal.

15 Mzungu. Mzungu. Angalia! Mzungu. A white person, a white person. Look! A white person.

16 A rungu is a clublike weapon made from wood (often a root).

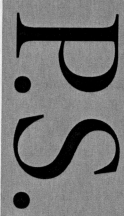

P.S.

Ideas,
interviews
& features ...

Adventurous Genes
Louise Tucker talks to Natasha IllumBerg

What did you want to be when you grew up? Have you always wanted to be a writer?
When I was a child I was busy being a child. Adult questions like the choice of a profession, etc., were for grown-ups in my world. I was far too busy doing important things like building snow-caves, sending ships of sticks and leaves on their hazardous journeys down streams, going fishing.

You live in Africa most of the year but come from Sweden. Where is home, and why?
Like a snail I carry the only place I truly trust on my back. I have memories from Scandinavia that entered my mind when I, like any other child, was an open-beaked beggar of the keys to all of life's mysteries. But when I was a child, and in my early life as an adult, land is what bound me to Sweden; now only friends and family do, and friends as opposed to land will agree to be met or to meet you anywhere.

When did you first go to Africa, and why?
I went to Africa to become a professional hunter; I have been living in East Africa since 1993.

You caught pike as a child and now you spend half the year hunting big game in Africa. Where did your love of hunting come from?
My childhood home was a hunting estate in southern Sweden.

You were a model before becoming a hunter. Considering your love of freedom, what made you choose such a controlled profession as a career, and what was it like?
I have *never* in my life been a model, and I am glad to finally clarify this after having read it in so many articles. Some silly journalist came up with this idea.

***Tea on the Blue Sofa* is a memoir, and yet you name yourself Anoushka in it. Was this in order to distance yourself from the story?**
When the book came out in Denmark I chose to call it fiction so I would not have to answer insensitive questions from journalists. But when Errol Trzebinski so kindly offered a quote, there was no point in pretending any more, and the book was published as biographical in England. To my pleasant surprise journalists were far more sensitive than I thought they would have been.

The book is in English and there is no mention of a translator. Did you write it in English or Swedish first? If English, how difficult or different is it to write in a language that is not your mother-tongue?
I speak five languages, but this was my first attempt at writing something in English. English is really a fantastic language if you are kind to it. Like a good hotel you can check in to English and expect it to meet ▶

❝ English is really a fantastic language if you are kind to it. Like a good hotel you can check in to English and expect it to meet absolutely anything you need or fancy without question. ❞

LIFE AT A GLANCE

Author photo: Isak Schiller

BORN

1971. Half Danish, half Swedish. Grew up on a hunting estate in southern Sweden. Later moved to Copenhagen.

EDUCATED

Schooling in the local village, then Copenhagen, and finally boarding school in Sweden.

CAREER

1989. Left for Africa as soon as she finished school. Worked on a game farm in South Africa.

1990. Returned to Scandinavia after a year, with the intention of getting an education in forestry and then going back to Africa later. Later became sooner. Moved to Tanzania after two and a half years. Tried to publish a collection of poetry (in Swedish) but was rejected. ►

4

Adventurous Genes *(continued)*

◄ absolutely anything you need or fancy without question.

Also on the subject of languages, you mention that very few white people bother to learn Swahili. How did you learn?
Luckily I learn languages very easily. I learned Swahili simply by working in the bush and having one book of grammar to help me form sentences correctly. But the most important tool for learning a language is interest.

In Africa you live and write in a tent. What technical and practical challenges do you face on a day-to-day basis compared with writers who take broadband and constant electricity for granted?
I have one solar panel and a battery that gives power to a lamp, my music and my laptop. When the African sun decides to give it a rest for a while, I either have to decide to do the same, or to continue on paper. To have the Internet at home is something I dream of. I leave the farm and go to town a couple of times a week to do my emails and shop. As far as research on the Internet goes, I have not stopped fantasizing about having the unabridged *Encyclopaedia Britannica* in book form yet.

Your parents ate a tiger's heart in India and your grandparents spent time there as well. Who most inspired your love of travel?
It is difficult to know which part of one's behaviour is genetic and which part is milieu. I think most children are adventurous and

would like to hunt buffaloes and live in a tent in Africa. But most parents would just smile overbearingly at their teenager when he or she told them such a thing. But one thing is for sure – with a history of eccentric and adventurous ancestors (both men and women) you can get away with a lot of things.

Are there any books that you wish you had written?
Yes, the ones that I won't live long enough to write.

Who are your influences as a writer?
I am really not sure. From reading books I get moods, not ideas.

What are you writing now?
I have just finished a novel. Its working title is *So Wanton a God*. It is set in Europe and Africa and has three main characters, who are all at tangents to each other and to erotic love. It follows a painter, a professional hunter and a bullfighter who are all trying to deal with the confusing relationship there is between time and love, longing and love, pride and love. ∎

LIFE AT A GLANCE *(continued)*

◀ 1993–9. Worked and fought a battle as the only female apprentice professional hunter in Tanzania over many years and finally got a licence.

1999. Published her first book, *Rivers of Red Earth* (written in Danish but also published in Swedish, Dutch, German, Italian and Czech).

2004. Published *Tea on the Blue Sofa* (written in English but also published or to be published in Danish, Norwegian, Dutch and French).

2005. Continued to hunt and write. She has finished writing *So Wanton a God*, a novel to be published in Denmark in the autumn.

FAMILY

Mother, one sister and her family who all live in the Swedish countryside. Father who lives in Spain.

Top Ten Books

This is a list undergoing constant change, but this week:

1. **Steppenwolf**
   Hermann Hesse

2. **Interviews with Francis Bacon: The Brutality of Fact**
   David Sylvester

3. **Crime and Punishment**
   Fyodor Dostoevsky

4. **Love Is a Dog from Hell**
   Charles Bukowski

5. **Sexus**
   Henry Miller

6. **The Master and Margarita**
   Mikhail Bulgakov

7. **Downfall: A Love Story**
   Per Olov Enquist

8. **Of Human Bondage**
   Somerset Maugham

9. **The Picture of Dorian Gray**
   Oscar Wilde

10. **The Brothers Lionheart**
    Astrid Lindgren

A Writing Life

When do you write?
Afternoons and evenings.

Where do you write?
Most of my writing time is in my tent in Tanzania, but I am really able to write almost anywhere if I have had three or four days to acclimatize and find physical quietness first.

Why do you write?
I was born without mental eyelids. So much comes in the whole time that if I didn't write some of it down I imagine my head would explode.

Pen or computer?
Sometimes I write by pen but these days mostly by computer. There is something so wonderfully cruel about a computer. Seeing my sentences reflected back at me from such a soulless piece of equipment in alien letters makes me feel under constant and deadly quiet criticism. This is good.

Silence or music?
Generally quiet (bar the drumming of warriors in the nearest village) but occasionally I will decide that I need music. When this happens it will only work for a little while, because it has to be a CD that I know well enough that it doesn't pull me away from my writing, but that I haven't played so many times that it has begun to bore me.

What started you writing?
When I was about ten my mother left and ▶

> ❝ There is something so wonderfully cruel about a computer. Seeing my sentences reflected back at me from such a soulless piece of equipment in alien letters makes me feel under constant and deadly quiet criticism. ❞

A Writing Life *(continued)*

◄ then my dog ran away within a week. That was the first time I felt that words could be too big to spit out and that a pen was needed to relieve the pressure. I wrote a poem about being abandoned by my dog.

How do you start a book?

I don't organize anything, or write lists of what I am going to write, or how I am going to go about it. I just start with an idea and as I get older a clearer vision of wanting to try to be painfully truthful. And then I get on with it, starting from the top left corner of the page.

And finish?

A book tells its own story. I never know the last sentence until it's there, any more than I would know my own life from day to day. But I do always finish a book with a sense of both relief and anticlimax. There is something sad about finally killing the buffalo whose essence I wanted as a hunter, or closing the book that was mine until the last sentence.

Do you have any writing rituals or superstitions?

No. All my superstitions have gone into hunting.

Which living writer do you most admire?

I simply can't answer this question as I don't admire any living authors in comparison to the old timers . . .

What or who inspires you?

As much as I strive to be part of a normal society, sliding in and out of aloneness is

6 I don't organize anything, or write lists of what I am going to write, or how I am going to go about it. I just start with an idea and as I get older a clearer vision of wanting to try to be painfully truthful. And then I get on with it. 9

what brings out a more candid impression of life. How can one really look at a picture and constantly be in it? Still I need interaction with people, with many people, and for all sorts of reasons. The person who inspires me is the one who can be in my life and manage to find buttons in my person that release some kind of self-electrocution.

If you weren't a writer what job would you do?
I write half of the year and am a professional hunter in Tanzania the other half.

What's your guilty reading pleasure or favourite trashy read?
I sometimes wonder how many hours I have spent in my life reading the back of chutney bottles, cornflake packets, tea boxes, shampoo bottles, etc. Why do I do this? ■

That Fickle Chum Time
Natasha IllumBerg

I WAS HALFWAY through writing a novel when my life came racing down, like a gut-shot crane. Straight out of the sky, it crashed through the roof, shattering my writing desk, my mind, yesterday's tea mugs and my computer. Encumbering the floor with pencils, notes and old newspapers. It split my house and each piece of my furniture right down the middle, made sharp, sad streams of exploded flower vases, and splintered the bones in my arms and legs.

I woke up one morning and eight months had passed. Two thirds of a year had seeped away to the rest of the world, while I was far behind, still in the split second, the blink of a cockatrice eye, it took for a bullet to travel from the end of a barrel to the softest centre of a body.

With a mobile phone in the one hand and collecting runaway marbles, one by one, with the other, I spoke to my publisher in Denmark and told him that I needed to put the novel aside for a while, to write *Tea on the Blue Sofa*. In the novel I had already been trying to masticate parts of the ambivalent relationship that exists between time and erotic love. In *Tea on the Blue Sofa* that subject had to return again, but now from a different angle. I had given a big part of my heart away, not knowing it would later get deposited into the night, like a ticking clock thrown into space. Only the clock itself knowing about the 'tick-tocking' in eternal orbit.

All different tangents of time to life fascinate me. One is the idea of the 'diamond wedding anniversary'. It was always very strange to me, this idea of using time as a device to measure the value of one person's love towards another. Loyalty to one person over time, though it can be, is of course not necessarily an act of devotion. It also mystified me when people tried to understand the depth of our love by asking me superficial questions like, 'How long did you love each other before he died?' You can't measure things like this. How long does it take to be conceived? How long does it take to realize that what you put in your mouth was hot and not sweet? How long does it take to jump out of a window? It is not about having, but about knowing. It is about recognizing the back of a stranger from afar and having such a fervent longing to see their face, because you know it already.

But as much as something can walk into your life, it can walk out. Unless you cut its legs off by the knees (which is a method many use with great success).

The number of conversations I have listened to quietly, where people discuss the best ways to keep wanting to love a particular person, even when none of the parties are happy in each other's company any more. When love was just trying to have a quiet death in their house they kicked it back into life again. Like a tough old cur it gets up with a pathetic yelp, and shuffles around for a while yet again, until it has found a different place to try to die with a bit of dignity. As time grows between them they watch ▶

> ❛ I was halfway through writing a novel when my life came racing down, like a gut-shot crane. Straight out of the sky, it crashed through the roof, shattering my writing desk, my mind, yesterday's tea mugs and my computer. ❜

That Fickle Chum Time *(continued)*

◄ proudly. Being consistent, as opposed to honest, sometimes to the degree of self-mutilation, is hardly the point of life. It has nothing to do with honour and everything to do with the fear of growing and facing a world that is a myriad of endless possibilities, like a mad rabbit's burrow.

There are no promises between love and time, physical or emotional meetings or partings.

How long does it take to realize that the person you shared your life with was somebody else for the last ten years?

That love can change, or disappear altogether, does not make it false, it makes it as natural, beautiful or frightening as the elements can be. It makes it surprising or 'hell-howling' painful, but not flaky.

It makes love brave, not cheap, that it can give itself completely to its last quivering edges to a person it has still only recognized as a silhouette caught between them and a beam of light. For in these mad meetings we can ignore, not count, the meagre crumbs of time we have been parked on.

To cut the ropes of two boats and find that they end up on the same beach, purely by giving in to the natural force of direction and longing, is worth living for, whether for an hour, a day or decades. The rest, as I see it, is quite unimportant. For it is about knowing, not having.

I only understand measuring love in truthfulness and strength of emotion and sneer at time, that fickle old chum, as time sneers at me. ■

6 I only understand measuring love in truthfulness and strength of emotion and sneer at time, that fickle old chum, as time sneers at me. 9

If You Loved This,
You Might Like . . .

Silk
Alessandro Baricco
It is 1861 and the silk trade in France is
threatened by disease. Hervé Joncour leaves
his family and village behind and heads to
Japan, a country that denies access to
foreigners, to negotiate in secret for new
silkworm eggs. There he falls in love with his
host's concubine.

Love in the Time of Cholera
Gabriel García Márquez
Florentino loves Fermina but, since she is
married, their love must remain
unconsummated. Half a century later her
husband dies . . .

Out of Africa
Karen Blixen
Karen Blixen left her native Denmark in 1914
to run a coffee plantation in Kenya. This is a
memoir of her time spent there, written once
she had returned home after the plantation
failed. It was made into a film starring Meryl
Streep and Robert Redford in 1985.

The Green Hills of Africa
Ernest Hemingway
Hemingway's literary celebration of hunting
big game in the African bush.

The Unbearable Lightness of Being
Milan Kundera
A meditation on irreconcilable love, time ▶

If You Loved This, You Might Like . . .
(continued)

◄ and the meaning of 'being' told through the love story of Tomas and Tereza.

A Venetian Affair: A True Story of Impossible Love in the Eighteenth Century
Andrea di Robilant
Their love affair forbidden by their differing social class, Giustiniana Wynne and Andrea Memmo must use subterfuge and secrecy in order to meet and be together. In a true story spanning many decades, the author (a descendant of Andrea's) used the lovers' letters to research and write the book.

Death of an Ancient King
Laurent Gaude
Old King Tsongor's only daughter Samilla is to be married. The palace is ready, rose petals cover the streets and the official suitor, the Prince of the Lands of Salt, is on his way. However, on the eve of the wedding another suitor appears and claims his right to her hand. The ensuing battle will wipe out all their claims and destroy the world that Tsongor created.

Written on the Body
Jeanette Winterson
A sparse tale of love and loss told against the backdrop of the lover's cancer. ■

Printed by RR Donnelley at Glasgow, UK